FACE IN THE SHADOWS

Marilyn Ross

CHIVERS
THORNDIKE

This Large Print book is published by BBC Audiobooks Ltd, Bath, England and by Thorndike Press®, Waterville, Maine, USA.

Published in 2006 in the U.K. by arrangement with the Author.

Published in 2006 in the U.S. by arrangement with Maureen Moran Agency.

U.K. Hardcover ISBN 1–4056–3563–0 (Chivers Large Print)
U.S. Softcover   ISBN 0–7862–8198–7 (Buckinghams)

The text of this Large Print edition is unabridged.
Other aspects of the book may vary from the original edition.

Set in 16 pt. New Times Roman.

Printed in Great Britain on acid-free paper.

British Library Cataloguing in Publication Data available

Library of Congress Cataloging-in-Publication Data

Ross, Marilyn, 1912–
      Face in the shadows / by Marilyn Ross.—Large print ed.
         p.   cm.
     ISBN 0–7862–8198–7 (lg. print : sc : alk. paper)
     1. Large type books. I. Title.
     PR9199.3.R5996F335 2005
     813'.54—dc22   2005024587

To my friends, Ethel Barr, of The Colony, and Ben Ferguson of Saratoga, Kentucky and The Colony.

CHAPTER ONE

In the beginning Andrea Gibbs had felt it was just a lot of fun! But then, without any warning, it suddenly changed. And what had been a teasing romantic adventure had all at once taken on a new and sinister character. In a reversal dizzying in its abruptness she stopped laughing and found herself screaming with fear!

It was a shocking twist of events and one for which she was not prepared. Boredom had lured her into making the first move but the nature of the game had changed and so had its cast of characters and from then on she was left with no choice but to continue the weird adventure.

She was threatened by a ghost dating back to the reckless days of the thrilling thirties! A scary phantom figure from that era of Prohibition, early talking pictures and the big bands had reached a hand out from the hectic past to once again bring violent death to a series of pretty girls. Andrea was a prime target of the ghost known as the silk-stocking killer and found herself reliving the horrors of the past while frantically eluding danger in the present!

But on that pleasant afternoon in late March all of this was still in the future. It began in a most casual and innocent way, as a joke between herself and her girl friend, Martha. Or perhaps it might be more accurate to say that it began with an accident she had while skiing on the slopes of a popular Vermont mountain resort a month before—an accident that had left her with a leg broken in two places and a hip injury.

The accident had forced her to quit temporarily her glamorous job as receptionist for a talent agency and when her weeks of hospitalization had ended there had come the days when she had to remain relatively inactive in her tiny East Side apartment with its view of the Hudson. Except for scheduled visits of a therapist she had few callers and the time had been heavy on her hands.

Andrea was the only daughter of Phillip Gibbs, the noted Hollywood film director, who spent almost all his time in the Palm Springs area or in Europe. He had a second wife who was twenty-two and since Andrea was already twenty-four there was an awkwardness to her meetings with her father and stepmother which did not encourage Andrea to see them often. Her father, wrapped up entirely in his own life and doings, seemed not to mind at all.

Andrea's mother was known professionally as Grace Barry. Her mother had brought her up in New York, having been given custody of her in the rather messy divorce case. Andrea had attended a number of private schools climaxing in a rather disastrous year at Bryn Mawr. Her Bohemian upbringing which had included martinis and cigarettes at eleven had, along with her fanatical views about America's villainous waging of overseas wars, made her a conspicuous rebel on the campus. And her most heralded escapade of pelting the Vice-President with over-ripe tomatoes when he'd stood on the platform of the college assembly hall after a spirited lecture on the glories of aggressive militarism had left her a campus heroine but a washed-out member of the school.

Then Andrea's mother, a professional fashion reporter, had found her the job as receptionist at the talent agency. Andrea, with her finely chiseled features, Mona Lisa smile, and shoulder-length corn-silk blonde hair proved to be more devastatingly attractive than most of the agency's feminine clients. So much so that she drew some jealous and catty remarks from many of the actresses and models who came by the office. With the males it was a different story and she had a succession of exciting dates with some of the big names in show business.

Her most serious romance, and one that had temporarily ended all the others, had been with Robert French, the noted host of one of television's most popular late-night talk shows. It was with Robert she'd been skiing when she had the accident. The egotistical Robert had been all sympathy at first. Her hospital room had been laden with flowers and gifts from him and he'd visited her regularly. Then he'd tired and the next thing she knew she was reading about his romance with a tempestuous auburn-haired French singing star. She'd had a straight from the heart talk with Robert and as the songs so neatly put it, he'd walked out of her life!

At the same time her mother had chosen to marry a wealthy retired stockbroker and left with him for the Riviera. This left Andrea on her own in her New York apartment with a hip mending all too slowly. Bereft of parents and boyfriend she had only Martha and a few other casual friends to turn to for comfort. It was a difficult spring.

Then on that afternoon in late March her friend Martha had arrived at the apartment after work to join her for dinner. That visit opened up a new and exciting vista for her. And plunged into a venture mad beyond belief, though she wasn't aware of this at the time.

Over coffee the dark-haired, merry-eyed Martha had produced an imposing legal-sized sheaf of blue papers and holding them up before her had announced, 'I have here the means of finding you the one man in the world really suited to you!'

From her stretched-out position on the couch Andrea had stared at her friend in

4

bewilderment. 'What have you there? The discharge papers of some kook in the French Foreign Legion?'

Martha looked hurt. 'The French Foreign Legion hardly exists any more!'

'Neither do perfect men!' Andrea replied bitterly, thinking of her unhappy romance.

'If you'd just let me explain!' Martha protested.

She put aside her demitasse and changed her position on the couch to a more comfortable one. 'Go ahead. I've nothing to do but listen.'

Martha tapped the blue papers. 'This is scientific! The latest thing! It's from the most noted computer dating service in New York.'

Andrea's blue eyes opened wide. 'A computer dating service? You have to be kidding! That's strictly for the yokels!'

'Don't believe it,' Martha said firmly. 'I've used it myself and I've just met this gorgeous hunk of man from Alabama who is working for IBM. He helped schedule the computer used in this service and he says it is unbelievable!'

'Just what I said, I don't believe it,' the blonde Andrea told her.

'You'd be surprised how many people are using it,' Martha claimed. 'My man from Alabama would never have turned up if I hadn't filled in one of these forms.'

Andrea looked grimly skeptical. 'Knowing my luck I'd say the machine has just about run out of charming southern gentlemen except maybe a few over seventy.'

Martha leaned toward her and in a serious tone said, 'I promise you that somewhere among the cards in that computer there is a Mr. Right for you!'

Andrea eyed her wearily. 'I had a Mr. Right and he found himself a hot-blooded French singer. And he didn't need any computer to locate her!'

Martha showed disgust. 'Robert French! America's nighttime host! His big love affair is with himself! Forget him and give the computer a whirl.'

'I'd feel silly!'

'No need.'

'The best I could hope for would be to expose myself to a lot of nuisances. What kind of a man would try to find a girl by means of a computer?'

Martha at once said, 'A shy, intelligent, idealistic man who prefers to avoid the crass vulgarities of the normal courting rituals.'

She gazed at her friend in surprise. 'You must be quoting the advertising blurb!'

'I am,' Martha admitted. 'But just the same it's true. And since you're not doing anything else why not try the computer and answer a few letters. Who knows what may turn up?'

'That's what worries me,' Andrea said dryly. But in the end she agreed and she and Martha had a wonderful evening filling in the questions to be submitted to the computer for matching with the right man.

'Are you slim?' Martha asked.

'I'm a hundred and one pounds and five feet two in height,' she'd told her friend.

'Are clothes important to you?'

'Well, I almost always wear them,' she'd teased her friend. 'What is the computer trying to do, match me up with a nudist?'

Martha was pacing up and down in the middle of the living room as she tried to fill in the questionnaire. With a tiny groan the pretty dark girl said, 'They want to know if you like clothes better than most things? Do they play a big part in your life?'

'Yes.'

'I agree,' Martha said, marking in the proper X. 'In literature do you prefer Chaucer to Shakespeare?'

'I like Jules Feiffer better than either of them,' Andrea said with mock seriousness.

Her friend looked at her aghast. 'How can I hope to do this right if you won't help?'

Andrea laughed. 'Go on.' She had a way of crinkling her nose when she laughed which was extremely attractive. And her large blue eyes were always bright with mischief.

Not that she couldn't be serious when the occasion demanded. She'd been deadly serious in her opposition to the Vietnam War. But she had this mocking approach to things that she found impossible to be really concerned about.

Martha finally completed the questionnaire and had her sign it. Her friend told her, 'I'll submit this right away and who knows, maybe by this time next week you'll be in the arms of your Mr. Right.'

'I'm more apt to be inundated with a lot of letters from Sorry Stephens who daren't approach a girl in real life!'

'Wait and see!' was Martha's comment.

'What else can I do?' she said. 'With this hip, it will be another month or two before I'm able to get around normally.'

Several days passed and she forgot the whole business. Her friend, Martha, was called to the Philadelphia office of her firm to take over for someone who was ill, and this meant she would be away from New York for at least a month. So she was not on hand to nag Andrea about her computer approach to romance. Without Martha around to press the matter it slipped Andrea's mind, until the long, businesslike envelope came from the dating service.

Feeling wryly amused Andrea opened the envelope and found it contained a mimeographed slip of paper with a message along with an unopened letter with her number at the computing agency and her name typed on it. The first thing she did was read the slip. It was formal in tone and simply stated: 'Our agency has chosen this young man as the person most likely to be compatible for

8

you. It is our policy to offer only one individual for your consideration at a time. If the choice proves to be of little or no interest we will provide you with a second contact, and ultimately a third. After that our responsibility ends.'

Andrea smiled to herself at the primly stated policy of the dating service. Then she turned her attention to the letter. It interested her that while it was on personal stationery it had been typed. Almost eagerly she opened it.

The letter read: 'Dear Andrea; I'm most interested in the statistics provided by the computer concerning you. You sound an ideal type of girl with that most valuable asset, a sense of humor. I'm a reporter on the *News* and I'd enjoy meeting you and talking to you. If you like me it is possible we might be able to have the last laugh at this rather weird mechanical fashion of getting introduced. I'm thirtyish, brown-haired with serious gray eyes and a jutting chin. My weight and height are average and I have friends who say I look something like a young Marlon Brando. I graduated from Princeton suitable eons ago, I've had my by-line on several series of feature stories and I am kind to my dog. Hopefully, David Barry.'

Andrea read the letter over several times. She felt like a naive young schoolgirl. It was ridiculous to be taken in by a letter like that. Equally silly to think that serious friendship might come of it. And yet she was nagged by the feeling that if she didn't take the letter seriously she might be sorry. It was just too much!

Because of Martha she'd gone into this thing as a joke and now she was beginning to hope that this David Barry might be as nice as he sounded. He was probably fortyish, paunchy, with bad breath and a repertoire of dirty jokes cribbed from a *Playboy* anthology of the same. He just had to be dreadful. It couldn't be otherwise.

There were no addresses exchanged. This was a protection of their clients which the agency offered. They could only write each other using their respective numbers at the computer service. And to her chagrin she found herself addressing a letter to this David Barry. She knew it was ridiculous and wrong but she was doing it just the same.

And in due time she received a reply. David liked the tone of her letter and was more interested in her than before. He confessed to an unhappy marriage and a divorce but he was hopeful that with the right girl romance could be a wonderful thing. She told him about her series of exciting romances ending with her meeting with Robert French and its unhappy ending. They got along splendidly. On paper!

Andrea had graduated from getting around with a cane to being able to walk unaided and with only a slight limp. It was nearly July and she had the choice of returning to her old job or taking a holiday for the summer. She debated which she should do. Money was no problem for her; her father for all his neglect of her in a personal manner, continued to send her a fat monthly allowance check.

And the letters from David Barry were becoming more and more personal. He was now insisting that they meet and she was ready to agree. Even at the risk of a disappointment she felt they should see each other and find out if they were really so well matched or whether the computer like its older associate, Cupid, might be prone to error.

Now that the time for a meeting was drawing near she was caught between eagerness to know the young man and fear that he wouldn't measure up to his letters. Martha, still isolated in Philadelphia, made urgent phone calls to order her to get into action and confront David Barry. It was a time of crisis.

Finally they came to an agreement. Rather than come to her apartment they would meet at some pre-arranged spot. She had the choice of the place and decided on a small uptown restaurant on a corner of Lexington Avenue. It was a noted French eating place and she felt the ideal place for a first meeting. They agreed if it didn't turn out well they would not meet again. They would avoid the embarrassment of expressing their views about this at their meeting but would offer their opinions in letters to be exchanged after the rendezvous.

It sounded ideal. David made the point that he had to work late each evening at the paper and so could not meet her until ten o'clock. This was satisfactory to her since on warm nights it really only began to be pleasant after dark. And the little café served until after midnight. She agreed to meet him at the restaurant on a certain Friday night.

By a curious chain of circumstances she was herself delayed on that particular evening. First, she had a phone call from Martha, who was all excited about the meeting.

'Tonight is the night, isn't it?' Martha had excitedly asked over the phone.

'Yes.'

'You don't sound thrilled,' Martha said with a lot of disappointment in her tone.

'It's not the biggest moment in my life,' Andrea reminded her.

'It could well be,' Martha insisted seriously from the other end of the long distance line.

'What about Alabama?' Andrea wanted to know, referring to the boyfriend from that state whom Martha had found through the computer service.

There was a short pause and then in a doleful tone, her friend said, 'That's over!'

'No!'

'Yes. He couldn't wait for me to finish working here it seems and he was too cheap to

12

take the train or plane to come visit me.'

'I thought he was a dreamboat!' Andrea told her.

'He would have been if I hadn't been sent to Philadelphia,' Martha insisted.

'Your faith in men is revolting,' Andrea told her.

'That doesn't mean David Barry won't measure up,' the girl said.

'I've never worried about that,' she told her friend.

'Let me know how you make out,' was Martha's final request before she rang off.

Andrea had barely put down the phone when her door-bell rang. It was the woman in the apartment next door with a problem. Her range wouldn't work and there didn't seem to be any reasonable explanation for it. Andrea had to take the time to go in and look at the stove and after some examination found a burned-out fuse. By now it was getting dangerously close to ten.

She quickly finished dressing and then hurried downstairs. The restaurant was too handy to make it practical to take a taxi yet it was a fairly long walk. She made her way quickly along a busy sidestreet as she headed for Lexington Avenue. The night was hot and there were a lot of people out. She knew now that she would be at least five to ten minutes late but felt that wouldn't matter too much.

By what she'd gathered about David Barry

from his letters he was a solid type who wouldn't get in a flurry about waiting for a few minutes. It was surprising how well she felt she'd come to know him without ever actually having set eyes on him. A great deal of his personality had come through in his letters and she was almost certain that he was someone she would like.

His opinions had suggested that he was fair, honest and not afraid to back up his views. His attitude toward life in general was serious but in no way sober. He had a keen sense of humor and this, combined with a wide knowledge of people, allowed him to be objective in his viewpoints. His articles in the paper were knowledgable and interesting to read. She felt she would be very surprised if she didn't find David Barry pleasant when she met him in person.

And while she would have considered it silly and incredible a few weeks ago, she had to admit that she was beginning to think of him in a romantic way. He had caught her imagination so that he'd become a very real person to her. If she were never to hear from him again she was certain she'd feel a distinct loss. That was how far she'd come in changing her views about the worth of computer dating bureaus. She still wasn't convinced that they were practical but in this particular instance she felt that fate had dealt with her kindly. David Barry was a person worth knowing.

In a few minutes she would be meeting him. Over a glass of wine and dinner they would have the opportunity of discovering each other and if all went well it might turn out to be a most important relationship.

These thoughts were rushing through her mind as she walked rapidly along the crowded sidewalk nearing the café. She passed a fruit stand with the produce lighted for night customers and the pungent odor of the fruit pleasantly perfuming the night air. Next there was a small record shop, a discount drug store and ahead on the corner the café with its front brilliantly lighted.

Traffic was flowing down Lexington Avenue rapidly. She saw there was a girl standing on the corner by the café and wondered whether David might have arrived there earlier and queried the girl about whether she were Andrea Gibbs. She also saw a young man in a light sports jacket lounging by the entrance of the café and wondered whether it might be David Barry.

She'd barely let these questions pass through her mind when she suddenly heard the scream of a police siren as it came rushing down the avenue toward the cross street. Then she halted and cried out at the sight of an out-of-control dark sedan plunging across the street and leaving the avenue to bump up over the curb and onto the sidewalk. The car careened to one side after knocking down the girl and narrowly missing the young man. At the same time one of its doors flew open and a youth in a jacket went racing down Lexington Avenue.

The police car came into sight and went after him. Andrea and the other shocked spectators now gathered close to the scene of the accident as a policeman came and took charge. The officer bent over the prostrate form of the girl on the sidewalk and grimly ordered everyone back.

Andrea stood there in a stunned state. In addition to her horror at the accident she couldn't help but think that had she arrived on time she would have been standing in front of the restaurant where the girl had been when the car hit her. It was a shocking realization!

Now the man in the light sports jacket came to join her and the others standing watching the macabre scene. The young man said, 'They've got him! Picked him up on Lexington! He stole the car uptown somewhere!'

'The girl has to be dead!' an old woman cried hysterically.

'Maybe not,' a man beside her said, his face grim.

'That's the way it is! You take your life in your hands on the streets today,' was the comment of an old man with a lined face and long gray hair.

Andrea turned to the pleasant-looking

young man who'd been standing in the café entrance at the time of the accident. She said, 'You were lucky the car didn't go any farther. You would have been hit as well.'

He gave her a worried look. 'Yes. I know.'

Somewhat embarrassed, she asked, 'You're not David Barry of the *News,* are you?'

The young man stared at her. 'No. What made you think that?'

Blushing, she said, 'I was on my way here to meet him. I have never seen him and I noticed you were standing in the café doorway.'

'You've got the wrong man,' the fellow in the light sports jacket said. He didn't add anything more as at that moment the ambulance came up to take the injured girl away.

There was the clamor of the ambulance getting on its way and the shouts of the police who had now congregated on the scene and were taking charge of the situation. In the general excitement the young man in the light sports coat vanished. Andrea moved on and went into the restaurant where the two owner-managers were standing by the check room lamenting what the accident would do to their evening business.

When they became aware of her they gave her their attention. She told them, 'I was to meet a Mr. Barry here,' she said rather timidly.

The older of the two men bowed. 'Ah, yes. Mr. Barry. A table for two. Come this way, please, Miss.'

He showed her to a table in a far end of the long, narrow restaurant decorated with fine, colorful paintings on its walls. It was fairly crowded and buzzing with conversation about the accident. She ordered a drink and waited for David Barry to arrive. She decided that he might have remained outside to cover the incident for his paper and that was why he was late. But at eleven he had not turned up.

It was at five minutes after eleven that the restaurant owner came to her apologetically. He bowed and informed her, 'I have had a telephone message from Mr. Barry's secretary. He is not going to be able to meet you here tonight.'

She was astonished. 'Not able to meet me!'

'I'm sorry, Miss.'

'Was there any other message?'

The man shook his head. 'No. Just that.'

She couldn't understand it. For one thing she knew that David had no secretary though it could have been someone in the newspaper office who'd phoned for him. What really amazed her was that he hadn't given any excuse for his not appearing. It wasn't like him. In fact, since he'd requested the meeting, it was downright strange.

She said, 'I wonder if he's ill?'

The owner shrugged. 'I cannot say, Miss.' In his Gallic manner was the clear intimation that it was none of his business.

Andrea was humiliated. This didn't seem at all in keeping with the character of the young man who'd written her so many fine letters. There had to be something wrong. Something truly important must have detained him.

'What does the lady wish?' the owner asked warily.

She considered and made a quick decision. She'd had little to eat earlier, so she opened the menu and said, 'I'll have dinner by myself.'

'Excellent,' the owner said with a smile. He whipped out his order book and waited for her choices from the menu. When she had given them he rushed away to see they were filled.

All through her meal she worried about what might have happened to the young man and why he had been so late offering word he was not going to be there. And why he had made his message so abrupt. Coming after the accident it was all the more mysterious.

She began to ask herself if the incident might have been planned in some way and if it had been intended that she were the one to be struck down by the car. She should have been waiting there by rights at the moment it had happened. Had it all been a weird plot against her? And if so, why?

The idea struck her as nonsensical—after all, he had sent a message—and so she dismissed it. But she still worried about the meaning of the night's events. She could not accept that David Barry had just not shown up

19

and that she would never meet him. Not after all her anticipation!

She finished her dinner and paid for it. Then she had the café doorman summon her a taxi and she went home. She half-expected some message to arrive there but of course there was none. She went to bed with her mind filled with confused thoughts.

When Martha phoned her again the next day she could only tell her friend the truth. 'I never saw him,' she said. 'He didn't turn up.'

'Didn't turn up!' Martha lamented. 'I can't believe it!'

'It's so,' she said. 'He sent a phone message saying he'd been detained.'

'He'll surely get in touch with you today,' her friend in Philadelphia said.

'It will have to come by letter,' she said. 'Or as a telegram. He doesn't have my address or phone number. It has to be sent to my number at the computer office and then forwarded.'

'It's all just too bad!' Martha said sadly.

As the hours passed Andrea became more upset. There should have been some explanatory message from the young man and none had come. She searched the morning newspaper until she found the account of the accident. It followed closely what she'd heard at the scene. A young man had driven wildly down Lexington Avenue in a stolen car. At that corner he'd gone out of control and landed the car on the curb striking down a young woman who was there waiting for her husband. The police had apprehended the young man and the young woman had not been seriously hurt.

So that was that! Andrea indignantly put the newspaper aside with the feeling that she might have been in the hospital rather than that girl and apparently the mysterious and elusive David Barry would not have been concerned about it.

She waited some more and then decided on making a move herself. She knew where David Barry worked. There was no use in calling the computer service. They had made it clear it was one of their rules never to give out adresses or phone numbers under any circumstances. The success of the operation depended on this sort of discretion. But she could phone the newspaper that employed David Barry.

Placing a call to the newsroom took some minutes and a lot of patience. When she did get through the young, disinterested voice inquired what she wanted. She told the party at the other end of the line she wanted to speak to David Barry. The young man in turn asked her to hold the line which she did.

Then an older, harsh male voice came on and asked, 'You want to speak with Dave Barry?'

'Yes,' she said.

It seemed to her the voice held suspicion.

21

'Who are you?'

'A friend,' she said.

'Oh, a friend,' the harsh voice said warily.

'Yes. I was to have met him for dinner last night and he didn't appear,' she said. 'I'm worried that he might be ill.'

The voice on the phone said, 'He's not ill.'

'I'm glad to hear that.'

The man went on, 'Dave has taken a leave of absence from the paper. He left the day before yesterday. I don't know when he'll be back or where he is.'

'Do you think he's still in the city?' she worried.

'I doubt it,' the man said. 'He made up his mind fast. I think he had to go somewhere.'

It was another frustrating exchange as far as she was concerned. She'd learned nothing of value about David Barry's whereabouts. Only that he'd left on some sudden mission. So it seemed she would just have to wait.

Waiting proved a difficult experience. And then one day about a week later a letter arrived to temporarily lift her out of her depressed mood. But when she read the contents of the missive she was crushed in spirits again.

The letter was brief but to the point. It read:

'Dear Andrea: I'm so sorry to let you down this way. But you simply must forget me. Things have turned up which make it impossible to ever hope to meet you. Perhaps it is best that way. I'm sure if we had met we would have found it difficult to part. All I can tell you is that our exchange of letters has been meaningful to me and I'm going to be eternally sad that we can carry our friendship no further. Good luck. All my love, David.'

It was a crushing let down after the way the exchange had started between them. And she couldn't think what might have happened to spoil things. Had David Barry hedged at the last minute because he wasn't interested in a romance that went beyond the letter-writing stage. There were men like that and he could be one of them. She knew he had suggested the meeting but perhaps he'd lost courage at the final moment.

As she debated this in her mind she idly picked up the envelope and searched it for a return address. There was none. But on the front there was a postmark and the postmark was clear. It said Saratoga Springs.

So that was where he was! At least the letter had been mailed from there. It was possible he'd moved on somewhere else by now but she somehow doubted it. And she decided that he must still be at the popular watering resort and racing town. If she wanted to look him up and try and extract some kind of explanation from him her best hope was to find him there.

Without much consideration she made up her mind to visit the city and see if she could locate David Barry. Finding him had now become a kind of obsession with her. She would not rest until she did. So she hastily packed some things and rented a car to drive to Saratoga Springs.

It was a rather forlorn hope. She couldn't expect too much from the young man if she did locate him. He'd been fairly cruel in not arriving to meet her at the appointed time and his letter had held no hope for a future meeting. In his earlier letters he'd shown himself such a proper gentleman that she simply couldn't understand his baffling behavior.

Possibly she was making herself ridiculous in this pursuit of a phantom person. A few weeks earlier she would have ridiculed the idea. But now it was different. She had become emotionally involved through the exchange of letters with the young newspaper man. And she wanted to find out what had made him change his mind about wanting to know her better.

She drove along the expressway in the hot August sun. This was the warmest month so far all year. The car was air-conditioned, which helped. And as she drove she debated on why David might have gone to Saratoga at this time of year other than for avoiding her.

It was possible that he was a racing addict, hooked on betting on the horses. Many people were and he could be one of them. Or perhaps he'd gone to the small upstate New York city noted for its August race meets to cover some story. It might be he had some big sports event to cover.

But she doubted that. The newspaper office had made it clear that David Barry was away on a leave of absence. This meant he was writing nothing for the paper unless he sent in a story impulsively as a kind of freelance. It could be that he was taking time off to work on some book project. That might be the answer.

At last she reached the outskirts of Saratoga and she was at once taken by its natural beauty. Its tree-lined streets and ancient houses had a certain air of tranquility and past dignity which told of the city's history. She knew it had around twenty thousand people and the population was almost doubled in this August racing season.

There were plenty of people around but they did not destroy the air of genteel decay and sleepiness which had taken over the old city.

She stopped at a corner gas station for gas and asked the attendant where she might find a room. He looked at her bleakly.

'Hard to tell this time of year. Rooms are all booked ahead by the racing folk,' he drawled.

'There must be some hotel you can suggest,' she said.

He considered. 'Try the Ansonia,' he finally decided.

'What sort of place is it?' she asked.

25

His freckled face showed a scornful grin. 'Used to be one of the show places here. But it's gone down over the years. Now they only open it for the summer. They keep their rates high for a run-down hotel and so it isn't always full. And then some people don't like its reputation. There was a murder there years ago and a couple of other killings around there lately. Lot of folks here think the place is unlucky. That it's haunted.'

Andrea listened with some amusement and surprise. She could hardly believe the young gas attendant had meant to picture the place attractively for her with this account of it. Yet it somehow sounded exactly like the kind of place David Barry might choose to stay if he were anxious to remain in Saratoga unrecognized.

She said to the freckled-faced youth, 'Do you think it would be safe for me to stay there?'

'Oh sure!' he said. 'They get lots of people. And the place is run pretty well even if it is old.'

'From the way you talked just how I'd assume there were murders going on in it all the time.'

'No! Nothing like that. The first murder was way back about forty years ago and then a girl staying at the hotel was murdered two years ago and last season a maid was found murdered out back by the shuffleboard. But a lot of people don't even know about those things happening. Only us who live here.'

'In other words what the tourists don't know won't hurt them,' she said dryly.

'Something like that.'

'And the police have never found the killer?'

The boy said, 'They found the one forty years ago and sent him to jail. But the new killings have never been solved. It's harder now. There are more people in the city and they have cars to get around faster than in the old days. So it isn't as easy as it was then to catch up with a murderer.'

'That sounds reasonable,' she agreed. 'So aside from an occasional murder there you'd recommend the Ansonia Hotel.'

The youth grinned as he stood waiting for his pay. 'You bet!'

CHAPTER TWO

After paying for the gas Andrea drove on through the upstate city. Along the way she passed a large, modern Holiday Inn which appeared to be well-filled. She did not fancy this as a place where newspaperman David Barry would stay but she did plan to check every hotel and motel in her search for him. She hoped that she might be in luck and find him right away at the ancient Ansonia Hotel.

When she finally drove up to it she was amazed. The gray wooden building with white trim at porch and windows was set back from the road a little distance. The elderly structure was Victorian in style with lots of fretwork and other fancy touches to the woodwork. It was the kind of building which couldn't or wouldn't be built today.

It rose four stories above its neglected gardens and shrubs with bay windows gracing the front. There was a large side wing in a building which didn't seem to be open. The parking area on the left of the old hotel was unpaved. Its mixture of clay and crushed gravel was spotted with breakthroughs of weeds. There were only about a dozen cars in the lot and she assumed that some of these must belong to the help. Of course many of the regular guests of the hotel would have gone to the racetrack and taken their cars with them.

She parked her car beside a venerable Cadillac and strolled to the verandah and the hotel's unimpressive front entrance. A trio of female octogenarians with a group uniform of print dresses, white hair in nets and blue sweaters draped over their shoulders gaped at her from their line-up of rocking chairs on the porch. To the left a thin old man sat sleeping with his hands folded in his lap. He had sparse gray hair and wore a wrinkled brown suit of about the same color as his equally wrinkled, brown, weathered face. His mouth had gaped open slightly and he was audibly snoring as she went by him. Things at the Ansonia were more peaceful than she'd expected.

Pushing the screen door open she entered the lobby. It was of medium-size and smelled of moth-balls and stale cigar smoke. A few faded divans were spotted about in it along with some rubbery-looking tall plants in wooden stands. The desk was on the left and she at once went over to it.

In charge of the desk was a clerk who looked only a shade younger than the geriatric female trio she'd encountered on the verandah. The chief difference in her was that her hair was a mousy gray rather than white but it was still ensconced in the same kind of hair net. Her shoulders were slightly stooped and she had the look of a well-fed pigeon. Her print dress hung from a sagging bosom as she stood there by the hotel register studying Andrea with suspicion from small eyes behind pince-nez glasses.

'What can I do for you?' she inquired in a precise, cracked tone. It was obvious that the last thing she expected was that a young woman of Andrea's attractiveness would be registering at the hotel.

Andrea managed a smile and inquired, 'Do you happen to have a David Barry registered here?'

The old woman eyed her bleakly before moving across to a metal rack of the cards of hotel guests and checking it at great length. She returned to stand behind the register before attempting to reply.

Then she said, 'No, we don't have any David Barry.'

It was a disappointment for Andrea though she might have guessed that he wouldn't be registered at the first place she arrived at. It began to seem to her that the Ansonia Hotel was not the ideal place for her stay in Saratoga. The ancient, big building with its gloomy history was more than a little depressing.

She said, 'Thank you.'

She was about to turn and go out to her car again when the old woman clerk asked her, 'Are you the one who was supposed to arrive here Monday?' It was obvious she was still attempting to logically fit her into the picture.

Andrea, wondering if there might be some connection between her inquiry about David Barry and the girl who was supposed to arrive on Monday, decided to play it warily.

She said, 'Monday?'

'The hostess they were supposed to send us from Albany,' the old woman at the desk said in her precise, irritable manner. 'It's not the first time that agency has disappointed us and I suppose it won't be the last.'

'Oh, the hostess,' she said, still in the dark.

The clerk pursed her thin lips. 'The hostess for the dining room,' she said severely. 'We've been short one ever since we opened and it's high time the job was filled. Did you come to see Mr. Clayton about it?'

Andrea improvised on the moment. The job seemed a good idea. It would give her a reason for being in Saratoga as well as offering her an excellent chance to meet people. What better place to check on transients than as hostess in a dining room? Even if David weren't staying at the old hotel he might drop in to the dining room some time. And as an employee of the Ansonia she could mingle with the staffs of the other hotels and perhaps locate David Barry in that way.

She said, 'Yes. I am interested in the hostess job.'

The elderly clerk showed satisfaction at having been astute enough to guess her mission. She jerked her head, saying, 'You'll find the manager's office around at the rear.'

'Thank you,' she said. And she walked down the corridor on the other side of the desk and came to an open door on the left. In a small, square room seated behind a modest desk was a tanned, middle-aged man in a neat blue suit. He was somewhat overweight and his very ordinary face wore a look of resignation.

'You want to see me?' he asked her, his face coming alive a little.

'Yes,' she said, approaching the doorway. 'About the job. The hostess job.'

The man behind the desk stood up and she saw that he was short as well as paunchy. He waved her to an empty chair. 'Sit down,' he said. Then he sat again himself. 'I'm glad you're finally here. You know what the job pays, sixty a week and tips along with free room and board. We close in mid-September so you've missed the best part of the summer.'

'That doesn't matter,' she said. 'What are the hours?'

'We use one of the captains in the dining room for breakfast so you can forget about that. You're on duty from twelve to two in the afternoon and from six until nine in the evenings, except on Saturdays when the dining room stays open until ten.'

She nodded. 'The hours are all right.'

He gave her a surprised look. 'The hours are perfect! You been employed in this line before?'

'I know what I have to do,' she said. And she did since she'd been used to every sort of restaurant since she was a small girl.

The bleak face of the manager showed some curiosity. 'You don't seem the type.'

'I'm only doing it for my vacation,' she said. 'Normally I'm a receptionist in New York.'

He seemed satisfied. 'That explains it,' he said. 'Do a good job here and I'd be willing to consider you for our Florida spot. We've got a big modern motel in Miami Beach. Nothing like this old-fashioned dump!'

She said, 'I doubt if I'll be available but I will think about it.'

'All depends on you,' the stout man said. 'No one ever complained about Ernie Clayton being a tough boss. By the way, what is your name?'

'Andrea Gibbs.'

He wrote it down. Then he said, 'There's a form or two to be filled out. I'll have someone show you where your room is. You plan to begin work tonight?'

'Yes,' she said. 'I can be on duty for dinner.'

'Great!' he said. 'The guests have been complaining. Not that we have so many. But the few that are here like good service. This used to be a top spot. Getting seedy for some time but the owners don't seem to care. So I do what I can and that's that.'

She stood up with a smile, aware that the

interview was over. 'Thank you. I'm sure I'll enjoy working here.'

'Do the place good to have a young face in the dining room,' he said frankly. 'We have a pianist plays every night and then later in the cocktail lounge. And the food is still a cut above the average so we get some transients at dinner.'

She said, 'I have my things in my car in the parking lot.'

The short Ernie Clayton stood up again. 'I'll have Mike get them for you and show you to your room.'

Mike proved to be a wizened little man with horn-rimmed glasses who looked hardly equal to the heavy duties of a bell boy. He wore a shabby blue uniform with red braid that seemed large for him. But he managed her several bags with seemingly little trouble.

He also operated the elevator and took her up to the fourth floor. 'Most of the staff live up here,' he said disconsolately without looking directly at her. He maintained the air of someone harried by a vague grief.

She asked him, 'How many guests does the hotel have?'

'Less than fifty right now,' he said, studying the far corner of the elevator bitterly. 'I can remember when we never knew the house count to go below two hundred.'

'I guess times have changed,' she volunteered.

34

He grunted as the elevator came to a halt at the fourth floor. 'Only thing this place is good for is a first class bonfire,' he said as he lifted up the bags under either arm and waited for her to leave the elevator first. 'Fourth door on the right,' he called to her.

She went down the dark corridor with its moldy carpeting and decided it was the ideal setting for a murder mystery. No wonder there had been killings in and around the building. She halted at the door he'd told her. A moment later he was at her side laboriously wrestling a key to get the door open. It finally gave way and he led her into the room.

'Nothing elegant,' he said, 'but it's clean.'

'Yes, it is clean,' she said, grateful for this small blessing and not able to stop comparing it with her pleasant apartment in New York.

'You have a basin in your room and there's a couple of bathrooms along the hall,' Mike informed her.

She gave him a dollar which seemed to surprise him. It occurred to her that the tips in an establishment of this vintage would not be large or frequent.

The little man hesitated at the door to eye her unhappily. 'You're the new hostess?'

'That's right.'

The little man grimaced. 'Don't expect to get rich on tips,' was his warning as he went out.

She began unpacking. There was really very

little room for her clothes. She was thankful she'd brought along a lot of hangers as the hotel provided only a half-dozen. A pull curtain on a rack formed a closet of a jog in the tiny room's wall. She went to the single window and found that it looked out on outbuildings. It wasn't too grand but it would do.

It was five o'clock by the time she was reasonably settled in the room. She went down to the bathroom and had a shower and then returned to her room and dressed. She chose a gown of fairly modest lines though it had a fashionable low-cut back. It was the most quiet thing in her entire wardrobe she realized with dismay, at least it was in the way of evening wear. She had plenty of nice little day-time dresses and sports outfits.

By the time she went downstairs with a gloomy Mike operating the elevator there were a few people stirring in the lobby. Perhaps a dozen older men and women were in sight. She crossed directly to the entrance of the dining room and was greeted there by a brisk, older woman in a white smock. The woman said, 'I'm Edna Savoy, the captain. I believe you're Miss Gibbs, our new hostess?'

Andrea smiled. 'That's right. I'll need some help from you at the start. I haven't done much of this work before.'

The tiny, slim woman studied her with sharp eyes. 'You'll catch on quick enough. It isn't hard here. We don't get all that much business. I'll show you around.'

With Edna as her guide she explored the dining room. It was high-ceilinged and paneled in the old-fashioned way with a number of heavy square pillars in it. The tables were round and all had white cloths and good silver and china on them. A tiny vase of wild flowers was placed in the center of every table. Only the rugs showed wear and gave the room a rather shabby appearance. Otherwise it was pleasant in the manner of fifty years earlier.

Edna paused in the middle of the softly lighted room. 'The kitchen is in the rear. We need artificial lighting almost all the day. And we have a pianist who begins to play at six and plays at intervals until nine.'

She saw the grand piano with music on its rack at the inner wall of the dining room. And she asked the white-haired Edna, 'Have you been here long?'

'Since the Carter Company took over the place thirty years ago,' Edna said proudly, her menus on her arm. 'I work in the Miami Beach motel in the other seasons. And I can tell you it's a lot different from here. We're really busy.'

'So I've heard,' she said.

'The waitresses are all college kids and so are the bus boys,' Edna said. She passed the menus to Andrea. 'You'll be giving these out and showing people to their tables. I have a plan drawn of the regulars so you'll know where to seat them.'

By the time she'd studied the plan and memorized the names and locations of the tables it was almost time to open the dining room. She was standing in conversation with Edna when a dapper young man in a white dinner jacket and black tie came to join them.

Edna at once introduced them. Saying, 'Miss Andrea Gibbs, our new hostess, meet Monty Freeman, our pianist.'

Monty had a round, tanned, pleasant face and curly chestnut, hair. He shook hands warmly with Andrea and told her, 'We've needed a hostess badly.'

'I hope I can manage,' she told him and now that the moment of beginning work was at hand she was really nervous.

'You can't miss,' he assured her. 'We'll have a talk later.' And he went on in to the piano.

Edna glanced over her shoulder and saw a group of the older ladies converging on the dining room entrance. With a sigh, she said, 'That's our cue to ring up the curtain. They watch the clock and get here each evening on the dot of six.'

Andrea braced herself for the onslaught, her knees feeling a trifle wobbly. But for the most part the old ladies and gentlemen were meek and polite and gave her no trouble. She got them all to their proper seats with the exception of one rather hostile type who at

38

once pointed out where her table actually was. Andrea quickly corrected her error and reseated the woman with apologies.

By this time Monty Freeman was playing a very pleasant selection of dinner music. She stood with Edna at the entrance to the dining room for a brief few minutes between guests arriving and saw a small, very thin man with a long, sad face and large brown eyes with deep circles under them. His hair was slicked back and thinning at the temples.

The tiny man who was more than a head shorter than Andrea halted at the entrance to the dining room. In a harsh voice he asked Edna, 'Has Cal Wayne come in yet?'

'No,' Edna said with a smile. 'But our new hostess, Miss Gibbs, can show you to your table and then send Mr. Wayne in to join you when he arrives.'

The little man glanced up at Andrea in surprise. 'Sure,' he said. 'That will be okay with me.'

She showed him to his table near the front windows and saw that a waitress was looking after him before she left. When she returned to stand with Edna, the older woman informed her, 'That is Slim Gordon. You must have heard about him.'

'I don't think so.'

'He's a famous jockey. Rode Silverstreak at the Kentucky Derby a few years ago. He still rides for the best stables.'

Andrea nodded. 'Now I think I remember. He won a big purse for the owners, didn't he?'

'He's won a lot of them,' the captain said. 'You'll know Cal Wayne when he gets here. He is solidly built, has a squarish face, with black hair parted on the side and wears dark glasses.'

'I'll try to spot him,' Andrea promised as the captain left her to supervise some table duties.

It was perhaps five minutes later that a young man arrived answering Edna's description. Andrea greeted him with a smile and asked, 'Mr. Wayne?'

He nodded. 'Yes. 'I'm Cal Wayne. Why?' He had a pleasant, manly voice and the eyes behind the dark glasses were fixed on her.

'Mr. Gordon is at his table waiting for you,' she said.

'Slim?' the young man said. 'Good.'

She escorted him to the jockey's table and then went to greet several other transient patrons and find them tables. It was almost always easy to tell the transients from the hotel guests since they were usually younger. It was some time before she had a chance to speak with Edna again.

Then she asked, 'Who is Cal Wayne?'

Edna glanced at the jockey's table. 'The dark glasses?'

'Yes. He seems interesting.'

'I don't know about him,' the older woman admitted. 'He has only shown up here lately. And he seems to be a close friend of Slim

40

Gordon's. I'd guess this Wayne is either a trainer or some kind of gambler.'

'You're probably right,' Andrea agreed, watching the two men talking earnestly over their dinners.

'You get all sorts of types in this place during the summer,' Edna warned her. 'Racing draws a very mixed group of people to a city.'

Around eight o'clock Monty Freeman came out to join her in the broad entrance way to the dining room and light a cigarette while he took a rest from playing.

The good-looking young musician smiled at her. 'How are you making out?'

'Not too badly,' she said. 'I haven't earned much in tips but no one seems to have actually resented the way I've handled things.'

'I've been watching you,' Monty said. 'It's hard to believe you aren't an experienced dining room hostess. You're a natural.'

She smiled. 'Thanks. I need to hold the job.'

'You will,' Monty assured her. 'I saw the manager, Clayton, watching you from the hallway and he looked pleased.'

'I didn't know.'

The pianist asked her. 'What are you doing later?'

'Later?'

'When you've finished work.'

She hesitated. 'I don't know. I have something rather important I want to do.'

'Oh?'

41

'Yes. I'm looking for someone. That's really why I'm here in Saratoga. His name is David Barry, and he's a newspaperman. At least he was.'

Monty Freeman's eyebrows raised. 'David Barry? You think he is here in town?'

'Yes.'

'What does he look like?'

'I don't know,' she admitted with some embarrassment.

'You're going to a lot of trouble trying to find him and you don't know what he looks like? I thought you must be old friends or sweethearts.'

She blushed. 'It's a long story.'

He glanced at his watch. 'I can't hear it now. I've got to play again. But why don't you take a table in the lounge after you close up the dining room. I take fairly long breaks there and we can talk.'

'I'll see,' she said.

'You can't go tramping around in the night looking for that fellow,' the pianist said. 'Let it go until the day at least.'

She smiled ruefully. 'I don't want to lose any time. He may decide to move on.'

'Perhaps he has moved on,' the pianist said. 'In any case a lot of people drop by the lounge at night. It's the only part of the hotel that really makes money. If he is in town the chances are he'll be coming into the lounge sooner or later. You could do worse than trying there the first night.'

She said, 'You've almost convinced me.'

'I'm giving you my best advice,' he assured her. 'I'll let the bartenders know you're looking for a David Barry. They often are able to locate people.'

'Thanks,' she said, heartened by his offer.

She remained on duty until all the diners had left the big paneled room. The jockey, Slim Gordon, and his friend with the dark glasses, Cal Wayne, were the last to leave. And she noticed that they went on to the lounge and took stools together at the bar. They evidently had a lot to talk about.

She went over the receipts with Edna and while they were seated at a table, checking on the customer count a big, gaunt man with a limp, wearing the uniform of a hotel service man, came into the dining room.

He was bald with a hollow-cheeked face and had a gray mustache. He wore dark-rimmed glasses and his eyes were blue and friendly. When he spoke it was with the lilt of a Scandinavian.

He asked, 'Could I work on the chandeliers now?'

Edna glanced up from the table and said, 'Yes. Go ahead, Olaf. Sorry to keep you waiting so long.'

'No trouble,' the big man said genially. 'I'll fetch a ladder. There are bulbs out in all the chandeliers.' And he limped away and out the rear door.

Edna told Andrea, 'That was Olaf. He's one of the handymen. Old for a lot of the heavy work around here. But he's been here every summer for three or four years. I like him.'

'He seems very friendly.'

'Olaf Bergen,' Edna said. 'They tell me he lives in a little room not far from the furnace room. It can't be very pleasant. It's so old and neglected down there. Mr. Clayton tried to get him to move to the fourth floor with the rest of us but he wouldn't. He's a very shy man.'

They finished going over the evening's accounts and then Andrea followed Monty Freeman's suggestion and crossed the almost deserted lobby to the lounge. The waiter there seemed to know who she was and found her a table for two not far from the piano. She sat there and Monty smiled her way as he continued to play the piano. She ordered a drink and sat back to relax.

It had been a strange afternoon and evening. She'd suddenly found herself taking a job she'd never intended in a place she'd not heard of until a few hours ago. Already she had worked one evening and made quite a few friends. And she saw that Monty was right. The dark lounge was crowded with people. It was the busiest spot in the old hotel and if he'd tipped off the bartenders she was looking for David Barry perhaps she might have some unexpected luck and find him.

44

She sat with her drink listening to Monty's playing and the buzz of conversation from the crowd in the room. And she began to worry that perhaps she'd made the journey to Saratoga on a fool's errand. That David Barry simply didn't wish to go through with meeting her and so had taken an easy way out. But remembering the sincerity of his letters she found herself doubting this. She was beginning to think that perhaps he was mixed up in some sort of trouble and didn't want to involve her. Reporters often got mixed up in various dangers. Perhaps she shouldn't be too quick to judge him.

Monty Freeman stopped playing and switched on the room's recorded sound system. Then he left the piano and after shaking hands with several people at tables near the piano came to join her. The curly haired young man sat opposite her and signalled the waiter to serve them.

Studying her, he said, 'So you took my advice after all?'

'Yes. Did you tell the bartenders?'

'That you're looking for David Barry? I did.'

'Do you think they'll be able to help?'

He shrugged. 'Who knows? There's a good chance. I asked them to give the name out to some of the regulars. He might be a friend of someone who comes in here.'

'True,' she sighed. 'The place is full.'

'I told you.'

She smiled at him as the waiter brought them drinks. 'You play very well. Do you work in the Miami motel during the rest of the year like most of the others?'

He shook his head. 'No. I'm new.'

'You must have had some lounge experience,' she insisted.

'In New York.'

'Where?'

He hesitated. 'Different spots. I'm not interesting. Let's talk about you instead.'

For some reason he had no wish to tell her anything about himself. It made her wonder. Again she thought of the many Mafia types who came around the racetracks in season. Perhaps this young man had been employed in some of their places and didn't want to talk about his background for that reason.

She said, 'I'm nobody special.'

'Nobody special in search of a David Barry,' he said in a mocking fashion.

'I work in a talent agency in New York.'

'Like it?'

'I suppose so. It gets tiresome after a while.'

The young pianist said, 'So does nearly everything.'

'So they tell me.'

'Where does David Barry fit in the picture?'

Again she hesitated to tell him the facts. She said, 'I happened to have had some correspondence with him. I think I might like him if I met him.'

Monty eyed her with his head to one side. 'Interesting.'

'Not really. We lost touch with one another.'

'Without ever meeting?'

'Yes.'

'And now what?'

She said, 'The last letter I had from him was from Saratoga. Only a few days ago.'

'So you think he is still here?'

'I hope so.'

Monty smiled. 'Let the bartenders work on it for you. Before the evening is over you may be in David Barry's arms!'

'I wasn't planning anything that romantic,' she protested. 'But I would like to locate him.'

'What made you pick the old Ansonia as a headquarters?'

'Most of the others are filled.'

'That's a good enough reason,' he admitted, sipping his drink. 'And why did you take the hostess job?'

'I thought it might help me. I'd meet people like you who knew the city. I took the job on the spur of the moment.'

He smiled at her. 'I'm glad you did.'

'I hope it works out.'

'What if you don't locate this Barry?'

'I'll leave. That's the only reason I'm here.'

The young pianist said, 'Maybe you'll find other reasons for remaining.'

'I doubt it.'

He said, 'What do you think of our spooky

old hotel?'

'It's rather marvellous in its way,' she said.

'You can believe it,' he assured her. 'If I told you the list of people who lived here in its heyday you'd be startled. Stage stars, society leaders, even presidents. Of course the trouble began shortly after the hotel had hit its peak. I understand that by the nineteen-thirties it was beginning to get a little shabby. And that's when the famous silk-stocking murder took place here. They say it seemed to throw a dark shadow over the hotel, and from then on it began a downhill slide until it reached the point of dejection you see it in today.'

She frowned across at him in the shadows. 'The silk-stocking murders?'

'Yes. Haven't you heard the story?'

'Not really.'

'I haven't time to tell you it all,' Monty said. 'I'm due back at the piano in five minutes. But I'll give you some of it. A pretty girl was throttled in her room here with one of her own silk stockings. She was the daughter of a railroad tycoon and the murder made all the newspaper headlines. The police came in and decided she'd been killed by one of the help. They worked on the case for some time before they pinned the guilt on a deaf and dumb man working in the furnace room. There were several suspects but he had no alibi.'

'How awful!'

'It was,' Monty Freeman agreed. 'There was

48

special sympathy for him because of his affliction and also because he had a wife and two normal children. They appealed and he escaped the death penalty but went to prison for life. He died there two years later.'

Andrea said, 'And that was the beginning of the legend about the silk-stocking murderer?'

'Yes. People began to say they saw the ghost of the killer in the corridors. Some of them even claimed to have seen the dead girl. The newspapers again seized on the ghost stories to make headlines of them and the reputation of the hotel really suffered. But that's not the end.'

'Go on,' she begged him.

'Two years ago another young girl guest was found murdered in her room. This time it was no one of any great importance, the showgirl friend of a racetrack gambler. But the thing which was to catch the newspapers' attention was the fact she was also throttled with an old-fashioned silk stocking just as that other girl had been some forty years earlier. It underlined the legend of the ghost of the killer stalking the hotel.'

She stared at the pianist. 'You don't think this other girl was throttled by a ghost?'

'No. But the killer was never found and the stocking, the weapon of death, was surely a relic from the past.'

Sitting in the dark, crowded room of the hotel in which all this had taken place she felt

49

a chill shoot down her spine. She said, 'What do you make of it?'

'Let me finish,' he said. 'Last year one of the maids working here was attacked and killed while on her way home. She was found in a field by the outbuildings, also with an ancient silk stocking wound around her throat.'

Andrea gasped. 'Was the ghost blamed for that as well?'

'By some people.'

'You don't believe it?'

'No,' he said with a sigh. 'I have a different theory. I think some madman has come to believe himself the reincarnation of that long ago deaf and dumb killer. And it is this modern psychotic who has committed the murders.'

'That's a terrifying thought,' she said, her eyes widening. 'It would have to be someone who was familiar with the legend. Perhaps someone living in the hotel.'

'I know,' he said, too calmly.

'You believe the same person committed both crimes?'

'Wouldn't the silk stockings suggest that?'

'Where would he get them?'

'He has no doubt found a supply in some long locked trunk. It has touched his imagination. And, presto, we have this madman running amok and playing the ghostly killer.'

'Do the police think that?'

50

'I don't know,' he said. 'I imagine so. I only know they haven't made any progress with the solving of the murders.'

'So the psychotic must still be lurking in or around the hotel?' she said.

The young pianist rose with a mocking smile. 'Yes,' he said. 'Unless you prefer to believe that these new murders were done by the phantom. You'll have to excuse me. I'm due back at the piano.'

CHAPTER THREE

Monty Freeman walked away through the murky, smoke-filled atmosphere of the lounge. Then he sat down at the piano again and began to play. Her eyes met his across the room and she saw something in them which she did not quite understand. She would almost call it a haunted expression!

He played a sentimental melody slowly and without really catching the attention of his noisy audience. He didn't seem to care about that. His handsome face showed a faint smile as he leaned over the keys and produced the lovely music. She wondered what he was thinking about at this moment?

According to Monty's theory a psychotic was to blame for the last two murders at the Ansonia. Andrea thought about it. He had mentioned that the convicted killer who had later been a suicide in prison, had left a wife and two children. Suppose one of them had grown up with an insane desire to revenge his father and had returned to the hotel to commit further murders?

She was thinking about this when she suddenly looked up and saw that Cal Wayne had left his jockey friend at the bar and was walking toward her.

The tall young man with the dark glasses

halted by her table. A muscle twitched in his right cheek as he hesitated a few seconds before asking, 'May I join you?'

She said, 'I don't really know you.'

'I was in the dining room tonight. My name is Cal Wayne.'

'Yes,' she said, tautly. 'I remember.'

He stared down at her. 'I understand you're looking for someone.'

'I am,' she said. 'You can sit down if you like.'

'Thanks,' he said with a certain irony in his tone. She studied him across the table. 'Can you help me?'

'Maybe.'

'I'd appreciate it a great deal if you could,' she told him with some urgency. 'I do want to find David Barry very badly.'

'So it seems. Why?'

Andrea felt her cheeks burn. 'I can't tell you that.'

'Yet you expect me to help you find him?'

'It would be helpful.'

Cal Wayne leaned forward on the table. 'It might not be to his advantage.'

'I promise I mean him no harm,' she said.

'You'd say that anyway. For all I know you may be a jealous girl friend or even a deserted wife, trying to find him to put the law on him,' he stated.

'I'm neither of those things.'

'And yet you are keen to locate him.'

'I've told you that,' she said wearily. 'If you know anything I wish you'd tell me. If you don't, please go and leave me alone.'

He smiled. She thought he was reasonably good-looking. He seemed so but it was hard to tell with the glasses. He said, 'Do you find me so repulsive?'

'No.'

'Well, then?'

Impatiently, she said, 'If you don't know anything about David Barry I don't think we have anything to discuss.'

'We could try becoming friends,' the mysterious stranger suggested.

'I'm not sure I'm interested in that,' she said.

His eyebrows raised. 'No?'

'No.'

'Why not?'

'I don't know anything about you for one thing.'

'Well,' he said, 'if it comes to that I know very little about you.'

'You know I'm employed here,' she said.

'Only as of today.'

'What do you do for a living?'

'I cultivate friends,' he said with wry amusement. She said, 'That's not a way to make a living!'

'I disagree. A great many people make excellent livings just doing that.'

'You're making fun of me!' she protested.

'Not at all.'

'The plain truth is you can't reveal what you do to earn your living!'

'That is close to the truth.'

'Which means you must work outside the law,' she told him. 'That's why you spend so much time making friends of jockeys. You probably fix races and make crooked bets on them.'

The man across the table from her said, 'If I were really in that business and heard you talking about me like that the chances are very strong you'd wind up badly hurt.'

'Is that a threat?'

'No. I'm just trying to make you realize you have to be a bit careful in making statements about people. Especially people you don't know well.'

Andrea said, 'Thanks. I think I can manage without your advice.'

'I'm not so sure.'

'You're very bold,' she said. 'I could call a waiter and have him make you leave my table.'

'But you invited me to sit with you?'

'If I did I'm now inviting you to leave,' she said. 'Just one minute,' the young man with the glasses said.

'Before we break this up let me tell you I think I can take you to David Barry. I make a lot of contacts in my business.'

She hesitated, wondering if this was just some other kind of trick he was trying on her.

'If you know anything about David Barry, tell me. I think you're bluffing!'

'Which distresses me,' he said. He took a sip of his drink and used the momentary pause to stare at her. 'I can't promise to find this Barry fellow tonight. Give me a couple of days and I'll come up with him.'

'Is that a guarantee?'

'The equivalent.'

She looked at him uncertainly. 'What do you want from me for this help you're offering?'

'It's a little early to ask that,' he suggested.

'I like to know where I stand,' was her reply.

'That isn't always possible.'

'Then I'll have to refuse your help!'

'That would be a foolish mistake on your part.'

'I think not!'

'And I disagree,' Cal Wayne said suavely. 'It is very dangerous for a pretty young girl like you to be living here at the Ansonia.'

She gave him a sharp look. 'You think so?'

'What about the murders? The victims have always been pretty girls.'

'So?'

The dark glasses were fixed on her. 'You are one of the loveliest girls I've ever seen.'

'You're telling me I may be murdered. I'm not afraid.'

'You ought to be.'

She looked at him in amazement. 'First you

harass me about one thing and then about another! What kind of a man, are you?'

He said, 'I'm a special type who follows the races.'

'You glory in being evil!'

He laughed. 'How can you say that when you know almost nothing about me?'

'I'll find out,' she promised.

'Now I'd construe that as a threat from you,' the man opposite her said. 'My main intention is to save you from being another victim of that phantom killer. I'd also like to help you find your friend.'

She protested, 'I'm positive you don't care anything about me. Whatever you're proposing is for your own benefit.'

He nodded to Monty who was still playing the piano. He said, 'You've lost no time making friends with that piano player.'

She replied, 'Monty is a fellow-worker here at the hotel.'

'What does that mean?'

She faltered, 'It means—I know about him.'

The young man with the glasses shook his head in despair. 'Feminine logic! It always confounds me!'

'Meaning what?'

'Meaning that this Monty has only been here a week or two. He arrived here a stranger and very little is known about him. People are more familiar with my background than they are with his.'

She didn't attempt any immediate reply. He'd made a strong point. There was no denying that. When she had tried to query Monty on his background he'd deliberately evaded telling her anything.

She said, 'You seem to know all about him.'

'I wish I did. I don't.'

'Then why bring him up?'

'To let you see how illogical your behavior is. You accept him as a friend without really knowing anything but that he can play the piano and yet you don't want to allow me to be your friend.'

It was a good argument. She said, 'You're twisting things. Not being fair.'

'I disagree,' Cal Wayne said. 'I'm placing all the facts before you most fairly. Better than that I'll give you some direct advice if you like.'

'Oh?'

He fixed a grim look on her. 'Leave Saratoga!'

'I haven't found what I came for!' she protested.

'Just the same leave right away!'

'I can't!'

'You're placing yourself in needless danger if you don't,' the man with the dark glasses warned. 'It is going to get worse rather than better and your chances of finding David Barry are not good.'

'Just a while ago you said you'd help!' she protested.

58

'Because I felt you were determined to remain here. But if I can get you to change your mind it will be all to the good.'

She shook her head. 'I'm staying.'

'Here at the Ansonia?'

'I guess so.'

'Knowing about the phantom and what has happened?'

'I'm not afraid of ghosts and I'll try to protect myself against live killers,' she said bitterly.

'Which could be more difficult than you imagine,' the man across the table said. 'Why are you so stubborn?'

'I mean to find David Barry.'

'It may be he doesn't want to have you find him.'

'I don't believe that.'

He stared at her for a moment in silence. Monty was still playing the piano above the loud conversation in the background. At last the young man with the dark glasses said, 'You won't be warned off and you won't change your plans?'

'No.'

He sighed. 'Then I suppose I'll have to try and help you. Finding that Barry isn't going to be easy.'

'I don't need you to help me!' she told him.

'You want to go it alone?'

'I think I can.'

'You're not afraid of the legend?'

'No.'

'Or the phantom catching up with you?'

'Not that either!'

He said jeeringly, 'How would you like to find yourself with a silk stocking knotted around your neck.'

She grimaced. 'Don't say things like that!'

'You know it's happened before!'

'I don't want to talk about it!'

'You'd do well to consider it,' Cal Wayne said. 'And you can be thankful I have a thick hide. I'm not going to be turned off by what you've said to me. I intend to be your friend.'

Andrea said, 'I like to pick up friends and know all about them.'

He rose with another of his maddening smiles. 'You'll know all about me soon enough.' And with a nod he left her to return to the bar and sit beside his jockey friend again. After he'd been there a few minutes Slim Gordon turned and stared at her over his shoulder with a gloomy expression on his long face.

What were the two plotting about? And what did they know? She had a strong suspicion that Cal Wayne was a smart talker who'd learned from the barman that she was looking for someone named David Barry and had proceeded to use the information to insinuate himself on her. If so, he'd managed very well. At the moment she couldn't decide whether he was a friend or an enemy. He was surely a mystery to her!

Monty had finished his session at the piano again and now he left the small raised platform and made his way back through the crowded room to her. He sat down opposite her in the seat just vacated by Cal Wayne and stared at her with knowing eyes.

'You had company while I was playing,' he said.

'Yes.'

'What did he want?'

'He'd evidently heard I was looking for David Barry from the bartender,' she said. 'He offered to locate him for me.'

The good-looking Monty raised his eyebrows. 'Interesting. Did you take him up on the offer?'

'I left it open,' she said. 'I don't know quite what to make of him. He's very cold and aggressive.'

Monty glanced over his shoulder to the spot where Cal and the jockey were seated at the bar. Then he looked at her again with a wry smile. 'He could be a dangerous type. No one seems to know much about him.'

'I pointed that out to him.'

'What did he say?'

She shrugged. 'He talked himself out of it. For one thing he said that I didn't know much about you either.'

Monty Freeman hesitated as he took this in. Then he said, 'At least you know how I make my living. You can't say that about him.'

'Agreed,' she said. 'I'm almost sure he just used the David Barry thing as an excuse to come over and talk with me.'

'That's liable to be the truth of it,' the piano player said.

'He also was very mysterious in giving me warnings to leave here for my own good.'

'I could do the same thing,' Monty said. 'And you'd pay no more attention to me than you have to him.'

'That's right,' she said.

He stared at her with grim amusement. 'At least he's made the first move. It could be that he does know something about your missing David Barry.'

'I've been thinking the same thing,' she agreed. 'If David got himself mixed up with some gambling crowd then Cal Wayne may have run across him. You seem to think he is a gambler.'

'A hanger-on of some sort,' Monty said. 'This town is full of them in season. And he's paying pretty close court to Slim. That figures. Jockeys could be important to him.'

The Muzak and conversation at the other tables formed a loud background to their talk in the dimly lighted lounge. She felt it was an atmosphere aptly suited to the racetrack underworld of which the piano player was telling her.

She said, 'You make it sound as if racing

were a very crooked game.'

'Not at all,' he argued. 'But the gambling aspect creates crooked circles on the fringe of racing. I love the sport or I wouldn't be working here.'

'That's why you took this job?' she stared at him as she asked this.

'The main reason,' he said, easily. It didn't seem that he was under any strain or that he could be lying.

She said, 'Why don't you want to tell me more about yourself? Where you grew up. The places you've played in before. I'd like to hear about your past.'

The young man with the curly chestnut hair countered this with a taunting smile. 'Maybe I'll fill you in on all that very unimportant stuff one day.'

'I don't think it's unimportant,' she protested.

'I do.'

'You just don't want to tell me!'

'Say that's it,' he agreed carelessly. 'When did this Cal say he'd have word for you about David Barry?'

'In a few days.'

'I'd like to hear when he comes back with some information about the fellow,' Monty said.

'I don't expect that he will.'

'You could be lucky.'

She sighed. 'I'll admit that now I'm worried

about what I might find out. It could be that I'll be sorry I ever tried to locate David.'

'I hope not.'

'Thanks.'

'But if you do find that he's gotten himself involved with criminals be smart and leave here at once. This is not a town to take chances in.'

She gave the young man opposite her a searching look. 'Would you consider me in any danger from the silk-stocking murderer?'

'I've already answered that,' he reminded her. 'I'd say you are. You're staying at the Ansonia and you're alone. Also you're the right age and have the good looks to fit in with the killer's other victims. In plain words, you're the type.'

'That's comforting,' she said wryly.

'Those are the facts.'

I'll have to stay now that I've taken a job here.'

He said, 'You can leave anytime. You have no contract.'

'I suppose not.'

'I'm not saying there will be another silk-stocking murder,' Monty said. 'That depends on so many things. The killer may have left here or even be dead. But just knowing it might happen creates a kind of tension in this old place.'

She smiled thinly at him. 'Keep on and you'll have me believing in the phantom legend. I'll be looking for shadowy killers in every dark corner or hallway.'

'It could be a wise precaution,' Monty said.

Andrea glanced at the bar again and saw that the stools which had been occupied by the mysterious Cal Wayne and the jockey, Slim Gordon, were now empty. She said, 'They've gone, Cal and the jockey. While we were talking they slipped away.'

Monty smiled at her good-naturedly. 'You can bet on one thing—they'll be back. This is a kind of headquarters for them.'

'It is suitably discreet.'

'Very much so,' Monty agreed. 'Time for me to go back to the piano.'

She said, 'I think I'll leave in a few minutes.'

He looked disappointed. 'I'd hoped you'd stay down here until one. I finish then. We could go somewhere for a bite to eat.'

She smiled. 'Thanks. Not tonight.'

'Some other time, then?'

'Perhaps.'

'That's not too definite,' he complained.

'How can I be definite when I don't even know whether I'll be here or not?'

'You're right,' he said, rising. 'I'll have to be content with half a promise, it seems.'

She said, 'I'll see you later then.'

'Tomorrow. I'll be playing as usual.'

'Good,' she said.

He left her again and started in the direction of the piano. Along the way he was held back by people who apparently knew him at various tables. He paused to smile and speak to them a moment though continuing his progress to the piano. It was evident that even in the short time he'd been playing at the old hotel he'd made a lot of friends. It wasn't surprising. He had a genial personality and he played very good piano.

As she remained seated at the table he began to play again. She exchanged a meaningful smile with him across the dark, smoke-clouded room. And once again she wondered if there might be an outside chance that he was David Barry. There were times when he seemed to know a surprising lot of information about her in view of the fact they'd met such a short time ago. And he had clothed his past in secrecy? Why?

For the time being it would have to remain an enigma. She could try sounding out the manager for information about him, but she wasn't at all sure that would bring any results. Perhaps if she were patient she'd find out eventually. In the meantime her search for David Barry would continue.

Before she reported to work at noon she would make a round of the various hotels and see if in any of them there was a David Barry registered. It was a tedious and probably unrewarding task she'd set for herself but one she must do if she were to feel she'd made a thorough search for the young man who'd vanished in this shabby old city dedicated to horseracing.

She left the lounge while Monty was still at the piano. When she reached the lobby it was empty except for the elderly male clerk working behind the desk. The lights had all been turned off for the night with just a couple left on to give the big area a murky atmosphere. It was while she was on her way to the elevator that she remembered she'd left her sweater in the dining room.

Deciding that she should retrieve the sweater she crossed back to the closed French doors leading to the dining room. There was a night light on in there so she had no hesitancy about going in.

She made her way to the small closet for employees' belongings just to the left of the entrance to the dining room and found her sweater there on a hook. She took it down and started out again. But as she did so she was suddenly confronted by a male figure blocking her way!

She gave a small gasp of fear before she recognized that it was the repair man, Olaf. Then she said, 'You gave me a fright!'

'Sorry, Miss,' the big man said. 'I have been working on the chandeliers and I saw you coming in here and did not recognize you.'

'It's all right,' she said, still a little nervous.

The big man stepped aside. 'I thought it might be someone come in here from the lounge. You never know. All kinds of people go in there at night. People you couldn't trust.'

'I realize that,' she said.

'I am also the night watchman,' Olaf went on in his musical accent. 'I double in doing maintenance.'

She asked him, 'Were you working here when the silk-stocking murders were committed?'

The big man standing in the shadowed dining room before her said, 'Yes, Miss. I had just come to work here. But I wasn't the night watchman then. The man who did that job died only last year.'

'I see.'

'Then they put both jobs on me,' the big man lamented. 'It is not easy. But they always try to cut down on help. And I need the job.'

'Did that other man ever discuss the murders with you?' she asked him.

He nodded. 'We used to talk about those things when our work was finished for the night and we lunched together in the cellar. He never saw anyone around the hotel on the nights of the murders and he believed they were done by a ghost.'

'Do you believe that?'

'No, Miss,' he said. 'I think the old man was not up to his job. He missed seeing the killer because he was incompetent, not because the killer was a phantom.'

'Have you ever seen anything you couldn't

explain?'

'Not lately, Miss,' was Olaf's reply. 'There have been no murders since I've been on the job.'

'That's comforting,' she told him.

'Thank you, Miss,' the huge Olaf replied. 'Just the same I would be careful. Strange things have happened in this old hotel.'

'So I've heard.'

'Lock your doors all the time,' Olaf warned her.

'I will,' she said. 'Goodnight, Olaf.'

'Goodnight, Miss,' the old Dane replied as she left him standing there in the near darkness.

She went out to the lobby again and was surprised to meet the white-haired Edna, who had just come in from the street. In her regular clothes the captain from the dining room looked younger. The little woman halted and greeted Andrea.

'It seems we are both out late tonight,' Edna said.

'I sat in the lounge for a while.'

'How can you stand the talk and smoke?' Edna wondered. 'I went to visit a friend who has a cottage near here every summer. I stayed longer than I intended.'

'It's not really late,' Andrea said.

Edna glanced at the big clock mounted on the wall above the desk. 'It's after midnight,' she said. 'That's late for me. I'm on duty at

69

breakfast every day as well as for the other meals.'

'I didn't know,' she said.

Edna called to the old man seated behind the desk. 'Grant, will you take us up in the elevator or do we have to walk all four flights?'

The elderly man said, 'One moment.'

They waited until he came around from behind the desk. He walked slowly and with a limp. He was a thin man with a bald head and a sallow, wrinkled face. He wore horn-rimmed glasses and had watery blue eyes with an uneasy gleam in them.

Edna asked him, 'Been busy tonight?'

'Nothing to do at all,' he complained. 'Not a check-in since dinner time.'

'We're having a slow season,' Edna said. She and Andrea entered the ancient elevator and the old man got in with them, swung the grilled metal door shut noisily and, grasping the control on the right of the door, started the elevator with a jolt.

As the elevator made a slow, creaking journey up the sallow-faced man said with disgust, 'They want to close the place so they're deliberately letting it run down. They don't advertise anymore. And a hotel like this needs advertising.'

'I agree,' Edna said. 'May I introduce Andrea Gibbs, the new hostess in our dining room.'

The thin old man gave Andrea one of his

uneasy looks and in a disgusted tone, told her, 'I can promise you one thing. You won't be overworked.'

Edna spoke up, 'We did a rushing business last night. One of our best.'

'It don't happen often,' the old man operating the elevator complained. 'And people will come here for meals who won't live in the hotel. Not after those murders they had here.'

'You think they hurt us or is it just the general run-down condition of things?' Edna wanted to know.

'Probably some of both,' the man said. It was easy to tell he was a confirmed pessimist. 'I can't see this place opening another season.'

The white-haired woman chuckled and winked behind his back for Andrea's benefit. 'You always say that,' she told him. 'But we still manage to open every season.'

'You wait and see!' was his final doleful warning.

The elevator came to another jarring halt at the fourth floor. She and Edna said goodnight to the surly old operator and then got out. The upper corridor had a single yellowish bulb hanging on a drop cord from the ceiling in the area of the elevator. This had to serve the long hallway which extended in both directions.

Edna started along with her. 'You mustn't mind Grant,' she said. 'He always has a sour outlook.'

71

'I gathered that. Is he an old employee?'

'Been here for years and works in Miami at the same job of night clerk.'

Edna said, 'This is my room so I'll say goodnight.'

'Goodnight,' Andrea told her. 'I'll see you at twelve.'

'My day will be long on its way by that time,' Edna said with a smile as she unlocked her door.

Andrea went on to her own room. Meeting the captain from the dining room had been a pleasant experience. It made her feel less nervous to know that the older woman had a room on the same floor not too far from her. And the conversation in the elevator had eased her tensions.

She unlocked her door and groped for the light switch. She turned on the light and entered the starkly furnished little room. She grimaced to herself at the meanness of her surroundings. Her search for David Barry had led her to a strange new environment.

Realizing she was tired she began to quickly change into her night things. Within a short period she slipped between the sheets and found the mattress under her uncomfortably lumpy. She also saw that she had to get out of bed to turn off the light in the room.

With a tiny groan of acceptance she got up from the bed and went over and turned off the light. Now the room was almost completely dark except for a slim ray of light which came in from under the door leading to the hall. She bumped against the dresser and finally reached her bed.

She got in again and pulled the covers up over her. She lay on her pillow with a sigh. From far down in the street below she heard loud voices and the sounds of cars starting and driving away. It was undoubtedly closing time for the lounge and its patrons were going their various ways.

She thought about Monty and idly wondered where the pianist would go for his late-night snack. She also again reviewed the events of the night. Was Cal Wayne to be trusted? Would he really try to help her? She wasn't sure.

And then in the darkness beside her there sounded a shrill ringing which made her start up in bed. It was the phone extension on the bedside table. Her hand trembled from the shock as she reached for the phone, wondering who it might be at this hour.

She lifted the phone and spoke into it cautiously, 'Yes?'

From the other end of the line in a disguised, muffled voice came the reply, 'This is David Barry.'

Her immediate reaction was one of fear. This strange voice coming to her over the phone in the darkness of the tiny bedroom sent a chill through her. Then she at once decided that it had to be some kind of trick.

She said, 'Who is this?'

'I told you. David Barry.'

'I don't believe you,' she protested. 'Is that Cal Wayne?'

There was an eerie low laugh from the other end of the line. And the muffled voice asked, 'Would Cal Wayne be able to quote to you from your letters? I can.'

This further startled her. She had never mentioned the computing service or letters to anyone in Saratoga and yet whoever was at the other end of the line knew all about her reasons for coming to the small upstate city.

She said, 'If it is David, why are you disguising your voice?'

'I'm not.'

'You sound strange!' she protested.

'I can't help that,' the muffled voice went on. 'I've called to warn you to leave Saratoga. To stop looking for me!'

CHAPTER FOUR

Andrea listened to the muffled voice on the phone with increasing concern. She said, 'Why are you calling me and telling me this?'

'I'm taking a great risk in trying to give you this warning,' the voice said. 'Surely you won't be foolish enough not to take it!'

'Why did you suddenly leave New York and come to Saratoga?'

'I can't tell you.'

'Why can't we meet as we planned in New York?'

'That's no longer possible,' the muffled voice told her.

'Why?'

'Things have changed. Just your being in Saratoga and looking for me can be dangerous to both of us.'

Andrea asked, 'How?'

'I can't explain. But I advise you to listen to me. If you don't then you'll have only yourself to blame for what may happen.'

She said, 'I'm working here at this hotel. I'm not going to leave until I see you.'

'If you stay here I won't guarantee that you'll be safe,' the muffled voice warned.

'Don't you have any wish to meet me?' she wanted to know.

'What I wish doesn't matter any longer,' the

voice on the phone told her wearily. 'Now it's a question of life and death. I don't want you in danger. Listen to me.'

'No.'

'Then whatever happens will be on your head,' was his reply. 'Don't persist in this foolish quest for me.'

Andrea begged, 'Please tell me what is wrong? Why you have come here? And why we can't meet?'

'I have told you all that I can,' the muffled voice replied and then there was the click of the receiver being hung up at the other end of the line. The phone went dead.

She gazed at it in angry frustration. 'Answer me!' she cried. But her question was only a mockery spoken into the dead phone.

Gazing into the shadows of her tiny room she felt she could break into tears. Then she tried to compose herself and try and make some sense of the frustrating situation. She jiggled the phone up and down to attract the attention of the switchboard downstairs. After what seemed an endless time her efforts drew a reply.

'What is it?' came in the sleepy tones of the man who looked after the desk and switchboard at night.

'I just had a call,' she told him frantically.

'Well?'

'Do you know who it was from?'

'No,' he said rather irritably. 'It came from

the outside. He asked for your room and I gave it to him. I have no way of knowing who it was.'

'You're sure?'

'Of course I'm sure,' he told her impatiently. 'Didn't I say so?'

'There's no way of tracing a call?'

'Not if you don't make arrangements first,' his reply was emphatic.

'Thank you,' she said, feeling defeated as she slowly returned the phone to its cradle. There would be no help there!

She wasn't even certain she'd actually talked with David Barry, and she was sure the voice on the phone had been disguised for some reason. The person had mentioned the computer dating thing but he might have somehow gotten hold of this piece of information. At the moment she couldn't connect that cold, uncaring voice with the person who'd written her in such a sympathetic and tender style.

But someone had called her. Someone had known she was at the hotel and even had information about her room. It could have been Cal Wayne though the voice on the phone had denied this. But he would be bound to deny it in any case. Or it could have been Monty Freeman playing a prank on her. Yet she doubted he was the kind to make midnight prank calls. And whoever had been on the line had sounded deadly serious!

77

That was what had frightened her. The warning that the muffled voice had given her. If by some chance she had actually been speaking with the elusive David Barry, why had he gone on so about danger? What did it mean? Had he become involved with some of the underworld characters at the racetrack? Was he afraid of dragging her into it and exposing her to the danger which would surely follow?

She couldn't decide. She would need time to think it all over. The phantom phone call had thoroughly upset her. She might have known she would get short treatment from the bad-tempered night man. Grant was a strange person. Her brief meeting with him in the elevator had left her with an uneasy feeling about him. Edna appeared to have grown used to him and accepted him for the eccentric he was, but Andrea felt less confident.

With these troubled thoughts crowding her mind she waited for sleep. Eventually it came and she didn't awake until the morning sunshine was showing in around the battered blind and flimsy white curtains of her bedroom window. Then memories of the happenings of the night before, including the phone call, came rushing back to her.

She sat up in bed with a forlorn expression on her lovely face. Perhaps she had made a mistake. Maybe she should return home to New York and forget all about this quest for the missing David Barry. Yet she knew if she did this, she'd always be tormented by doubts. She would always feel that she should have made a bit more effort to find him even at some risk.

With this in mind she quickly got up and put on her dressing gown. She then went down the hall to the bathroom to wash. The upper floor seemed quiet and deserted, so she guessed that most of the other help living there with her had already gone down to work. A refreshing shower helped make her feel more able to meet the day ahead.

She returned to her room and dressed. Then she went down to have breakfast. Edna had informed her there were tables at the rear of the big dining room for the staff. When she arrived down there the white-haired woman greeted her with a smile and showed her the tables.

'You look more rested,' Edna said.

'I had a very good sleep,' she told her.

'Then you must have a better mattress than mine,' the captain said.

She laughed. 'Not really. I think it was chiefly because I was so tired.' And she went on down to the staff tables. Only one person was seated there, manager Ernie Clayton. The paunchy man greeted her with a nod as she sat down opposite him.

'Getting settled?' he asked.

'I'd say so,' she said.

'You seemed to be doing just fine for someone with little experience when I looked in here last night,' he said.

She smiled. 'Thank you. I'll certainly try hard.'

'It relieves Edna a little,' the manager said. 'She's been carrying the whole burden all season and it's been too much for her.'

'I don't doubt that,' Andrea said.

The manager was studying her hopefully. 'You think you'll stay with us, then?'

'Unless something unexpected turns up,' she said.

'Good!' he said, showing satisfaction. 'There is always the opportunity of working for us in Miami as well if you should be interested.'

'I'll think about it,' she said, putting him off. And then she asked, 'Where does Monty Freeman work when he's not here?'

The manager frowned slightly. 'I actually don't know. This is his first season with us. We hired him rather hastily when the man who was to come didn't show up.'

'I see,' she said.

'He was playing in one of the smaller lounges and he heard about the vacancy and came over to see me about it. I was in a desperate spot so I hired him at once without asking any questions. He's not a very communicative type so I haven't learned much about him since.'

She said, 'He plays very well.'

'Yes,' the manager agreed. 'And that's the main thing.' With that he got up and left her alone at the staff table.

A waitress came and she ordered breakfast. There was a lull in the dining room and Edna, her sheaf of menus in hand, came to sit with her for a few minutes.

'I'll keep my back partially turned to you so I can watch the door,' the white-haired captain said. 'I don't think we'll have any more in for breakfast but you can't be sure. And I want to see them when they arrive.'

'Of course,' she said.

'What did Ernie Clayton have to say?' Edna asked.

'Ernie Clayton?' she asked, blankly.

'The manager.'

'Of course! I'd forgotten his name for a moment,' Andrea said. 'He didn't have much to say beyond telling me he was satisfied with the way I coped with the dinner patrons last night.'

'I thought he was pleased.'

'He seemed to be,' Andrea said. 'And he urged me to stay on for the season.'

'I hope you will,' the white-haired woman said with a sigh. 'I don't think I can carry on if you don't.'

'Mr. Clayton is aware of your problem.'

'But he didn't do anything to solve it until you came along,' Edna said. 'I can tell you the secret about him. He's lazy!'

'How long has he been managing the Ansonia?'

'He's been working in Miami for years but they only sent him up here two years ago. And he's really done nothing to make it any better since he arrived.'

'Don't they ever check on him?' Andrea asked.

'Not lately,' the captain said. 'They believe everything he tells them and he makes sure he protects himself.' She got up quickly as she added, 'Here come two of my late old ladies.' And she hurried off to greet them.

Andrea resumed her breakfast. When she finished she left the hotel and got into her car. Then she began driving around the old city. At one time it had been noted as a famous spa. It was still a famous health resort but now thoroughbred racing had taken the spotlight and was one of the main attractions for visitors.

She tried the Holiday Inn and found no David Barry registered there. They suggested she might try the Grand Union Motel. But a stop there also produced no results. After that she called at several of the smaller lodging places without any luck. She began to realize that this was not the way to find the missing David. Monty's method of having the bartenders send out queries about David had worked much better. It had even resulted in her getting that phone call whether it was real or a fake.

For the short time left her the rest of the morning she took in some of the sights of the city. She visited the Congress Park and Casino which had been a gambling casino built by boxing champion, John Morrissey in 1867. The park was landscaped with charming Italian gardens and sculpture by Daniel Chester French and Bertel Thorvaldsen.

She also stopped by the Drink Hall at Broadway and Congress Street to sample the famed mineral waters. The place seemed filled with tourists, mostly families, and not the sort of people one saw in the Ansonia Lounge after dark. She knew she wasn't going to locate David Barry in any of these places yet she felt she should see them since she was in Saratoga.

She made a visit to the National Museum of Thoroughbred Racing and saw the array of racing mementos and fine paintings on the subject. A final stop at Yaddo, a private estate with rose gardens, completed her brief tour of the city.

At twelve she reported for duty at the dining room. The luncheon trade was confined mostly to the regulars so it was a fairly easy work period for her. When she finished she had her own lunch and afterward wandered out into the lobby. Almost the first person she saw out there was the pianist, Monty.

He looked very different in his slacks and sports shirt. To her he seemed a lot younger looking in the open-necked shirt than in black tie and dinner jacket.

Greeting her with a smile, he said, 'I see you're still with us.'

'Didn't you expect me to be?'

'I wasn't sure,' he said. 'The turnover in help is heavy here.'

Her eyes twinkled. 'I'm not all that easily discouraged.'

'Not even about finding David Barry?'

'No,' she said. 'I'll locate him eventually.'

'I hope so,' Monty said. 'Sorry I wasn't able to be more help last night.'

'I have something to tell you about last night,' she said. 'Can we take a walk outside?'

'Why not? The old folks who stay here hardly ever use any of the recreation area. We might as well enjoy it.'

They left the lobby by the rear door opening on the large verandah which ran all around the old hotel. A few of the veteran males and females were dozing comfortably in rocking chairs as they passed them and went on down the steps to the lawn.

As they strolled across the lawn in the bright afternoon sunshine the chestnut-haired young man told her, 'I'd invite you for a game of tennis but the courts have been let go to the point where they can't be used.'

'More of the manager's neglect?'

'I suppose so,' he said. 'But you can hardly blame him since no one ever used them.'

'And you have no swimming pool?'

'That we definitely don't need,' Monty said. 'But you'll see just ahead there is a shuffleboard. And on the other lawn there is a fair putting green which a few of the mobile guests use occasionally.'

She laughed. 'You have no illusions about the patronage the Ansonia gets.'

'How can I have? I see them every day in their chairs on the verandah and in the dining room at night. It's a geriatric refuge. There's no doubt about that!'

'A few family groups and young people do come here,' she insisted.

'Very few,' he agreed grudgingly. 'And I doubt if they ever come back. The night man, Grant, claims they're about to close the place down and he's probably right.'

'I hear he's been claiming that for years.'

'I didn't know. Who told you?'

'Edna,' she said, approaching the shuffleboard. She glanced at him. 'Isn't this where that girl was murdered? The maid who worked for the hotel?'

A strange expression had come to the young man's pleasant face. He said, 'How do you happen to know that?'

She was aware of the sudden change in him and it made her wonder and worry some. She said, 'I was told about it, of course. How else could I know?'

'How else,' he echoed, still seeming upset.

She gave him a wry smile. 'Did you bring me to this spot on purpose?'

'No.'

'It would be a good object lesson,' she went on. 'She was the third silk-stocking murder victim. Where did they find her with the stocking wound around her neck?'

Monty said, 'I don't know.'

'It was somewhere near the shuffleboard,' she said, glancing around.

'Probably behind that hedge,' he suggested. 'That would be an ideal place to hide a body.'

She turned quickly to give him a probing glance. 'Do you think so?'

He looked flustered. 'I gave you an answer. You asked me.'

'So I did,' she said. 'I was startled that you'd brought me directly to this spot. This murder spot.'

'I hadn't even thought of it.'

'Are you sure?'

'Of course,' he said. 'I thought you wanted to tell me something. Instead, all you've done is ask me a lot of questions about that maid's murder.'

'The silk-stocking murders do overshadow the old hotel,' she reminded him. 'Don't you agree?'

'I think the whole place belongs to another age,' he said bitterly. 'And so do the murders.'

'It was only last year they found that girl throttled out here.'

He seemed upset but she didn't mind. It was one way of trying to find out the truth about him. Since he wouldn't tell anything about himself she was having to try and make him reveal his true character.

She said, 'If I remember rightly from our conversation you think some young criminal may be imagining himself the original silk-stocking murderer and doing the killings that have happened recently.'

'What motive would he have?' the pianist asked, ignoring her statement and staring at her oddly.

'Would he need a motive beyond ordinary madness and a knowledge of the first crime?'

'Probably not,' he said. 'I can't be certain how a madman's mind works.'

'No,' she agreed quietly. 'That is true.'

'Well, have we exhausted the subject?' he asked with a hint of exasperation.

'We have,' she said.

'Then let's get away from this shuffleboard since it seems to fill you with macabre thoughts,' he said, almost roughly taking her by the arm and leading her away.

'I'm sorry,' she said. 'I annoyed you.'

'Not exactly,' he told her. 'I just wasn't prepared for it. I had no idea you enjoyed the gory details of crime.'

'I don't as a general rule.'

'They certainly seem to appeal to you now,' Monty said rather sulkily.

'I'm sorry,' she said.

'We came out here because you had something urgent to tell me, if I remember rightly,' the young pianist said.

'That's right,' she agreed.

They had crossed to the other area of the lawn by the putting green which was also deserted. There were benches beside the green and they sat down on one of these.

Monty faced her. 'Well, what did you have to tell me?'

Now she suddenly felt uneasy. She hardly knew how to begin. She still wasn't sure whether he might have made the call or not.

She said, 'You didn't call me last night, did you?'

He showed surprise. 'No. Why do you ask that?'

'I had a phone call after midnight. It came from someone disguising his real voice.'

'You have no idea who it was?'

'No. The voice was muffled but claimed to be David Barry,' she said.

Monty was at once more interested. 'You had a call that was supposed to come from the missing David?'

'Yes.'

'Do you think it was he?'

'I can't say.'

'What did he tell you?'

She sighed. 'Not very much. He worked hard to make me believe it was David. And then he urged me to give up searching for him and leave Saratoga.'

'At least he gave you sound advice,' was Monty's comment.

'You think so?'

'I do,' he said.

She eyed him doubtfully. 'I don't agree. I have to find David. I'll never be satisfied if I don't. It will remain unsettled business.'

Monty looked grimly concerned. 'Sometimes it is better to leave certain things unsettled. If this David actually called you and told you not to try and find him he must have some good reason for it.'

'I'm not at all sure it was David,' she argued.

'He knew why you were in Saratoga and where to find you,' the pianist said.

'He could have found out those things.'

'Not too easily.'

'But it is possible the caller had,' she maintained. 'I think the call may have come from someone else who wants me to leave Saratoga.'

'For what reason?'

'I haven't figured that out,' she said. 'When I do I'll tell you.'

The young man looked baffled. 'Since you won't listen to any of my advice why did you tell me about this at all?'

'I wanted you to know,' she said solemnly. 'I'm trying to keep you up to date on what is going on so if anything should happen to me you'll know all the facts.'

Monty studied her earnestly. 'Nothing had better happen to you.'

She smiled forlornly. 'Would you really be upset?'

'You know I would,' he said, and as if to prove it he drew her close to him and kissed her.

Andrea pulled away from him quickly, her pretty face crimson. 'You shouldn't have done that. They can see us here from the hotel verandah.'

'Those old fogies can't see this far!' he scoffed.

'Don't be too sure of that,' she told him. 'I don't want us reported and losing our jobs.'

'You needn't worry about that,' Monty said. 'The hotel needs us worse than we need it. They're desperate for help and no wonder!'

She smiled at him reproachfully. 'You're impossible.'

'And you're not all that easy to understand,' he chided her.

She got up from the bench. 'It's time to move on.'

He rose with her. 'I'd like to have some more time with you.'

'Not now,' she said. 'I have a lot of other things to do.'

They began walking back in the direction of the hotel. She said, 'I hope the bartenders are able to get me a line to David.'

'I'll tell them to keep trying,' he promised.

'I don't know what else to do.'

'Don't try anything for a while,' was his advice. 'Pay close attention to your job and be patient. If David Barry is in town word will come to the bar sooner or later.'

'You sound very sure of that,' she said, looking up at him.

'I am,' he told her. 'Those fellows know everything that goes on in this town.'

She smiled. 'That means my staying around the lounge at night.'

'I like having you there,' Monty said. 'I play for you in a very special way.'

'You probably tell that to every girl you entice in there,' she teased him.

'No, only the prettiest ones,' he said with a wink.

They had reached the steps leading to the rear verandah of the hotel. She said, 'You haven't offered an opinion on whether you believe that phone call was a hoax or not.'

He hesitated. 'I don't know what to say.'

'I keep wondering if it mightn't have been Cal Wayne disguising his voice,' she said.

'That's a possibility.'

'I don't know why he'd do such a thing other than to torment me.'

Monty said, 'Say it was the real David Barry. What then?'

'I don't know. I can only say I was much more impressed by his letters than by talking to him.'

'Some people are like that. They write well and aren't able to make a conversation nearly as interesting. If David was your caller, that would have to be his type,' he said. 'He won you with his letters and lost you with his talk.'

'Something like that,' she said unhappily.

'I told you before. Be patient. That's the best thing for you at this point.'

That was the end of their discussion. They went back inside the old hotel and parted. She went upstairs to her room to get an afternoon nap so she'd be in better shape to last a long evening. She fell asleep almost at once and began to dream. In her dream she was pursued by a masked man. And when he came close he held out a single silk stocking ready to twist around her neck. Then he sprang forward and she barely dodged him the second time. Finally he slipped the stocking around her throat and as she fought to free herself she tore off his mask. The face she saw beneath the mask was that of Monty Freeman. She awoke from the dream perspiring and terrified.

Seeing that it was now time for her to wash and dress for dinner she got off the bed. Again she went down the hall to the bathroom to take a shower. As she was returning down the hall to her own room again she heard the creak of one of the doors along the passage.

The sound gave her an eerie feeling and she hesitated and glanced to see which door it was.

And she decided it was one almost opposite her. She went to it and knocked on it. After a moment the door was opened and the surly night watchman came out.

His eyes still blinking from sleep he tried to collect himself as he glared at her. 'What is it?' Grant asked.

She felt it best to tell the truth. She said, 'I heard your door creak open and felt you were watching me.'

Grant showed disgust on his thin face. The old man said, 'Maybe I didn't properly shut the door and it creaked open by itself. The motion you made on the floor in walking by would have been enough to do it.'

'I don't think so,' she argued. 'When I came over to the door just now it was closed. Before that I'd thought it had probably opened in the way you have described. But now I know better.'

'You can think what you like,' Grant snapped. 'You woke me from a sound sleep.' And saying that he slammed the door in her face.

She continued on to her room somewhat upset. She was almost sure he'd been spying on her through the crack in the door and when he realized she'd caught on he had promptly closed the door and pretended to be asleep. There was something rather sinister about the old night clerk and it bothered her.

Later, while she was dressing in her room,

she mulled over the phone call of the night before. And she recalled that Grant had been on the switchboard at the time. He could have easily made the call disguising his voice to terrify her. She also remembered that he had been working at the Ansonia Hotel during the times of the murders. Could it be that he was the killer?

Surely he was surly and bitter enough. But she had no right to jump to conclusions. It was likely she'd find out the answers to some of the puzzling questions if she obeyed Monty Freeman and patiently waited. By the same token she could also place herself in grave danger by following the identical advice.

Downstairs she took her place at the entrance to the dining room again for the night's work. Some of the regulars recognized her this time and spoke to her pleasantly as she showed them to their tables. She enjoyed this.

A few transients drifted in and she assigned them tables. The place did not seem as crowded as the night before and she mentioned this to Edna when they had a free moment together.

Edna's reply was, 'Don't worry! They'll be along later.'

And the white-haired woman proved right. It was a late-night crowd. Soon most of the tables were filled for a second time.

It was then that Cal Wayne appeared

accompanied by his diminutive pal, Slim Gordon. The two smiled at her as she greeted them.

Cal said, 'I guess we have the same table as usual?'

'That's the regular procedure,' she told him. And she rather self-consciously led the way across the dining room to their table.

'Thanks,' the tanned Cal said.

Slim Gordon, the jockey, was already seating himself at the table as he asked her, 'Were you ever in Vegas?'

'No,' she said.

The jockey's thin face showed doubt. 'I'm sure I saw you in Vegas. At one of the big clubs there. You were with another girl. A redhead.'

'You're wrong,' she said, not certain whether he was merely teasing her or not.

Cal Wayne smiled at her. 'Slim gets a lot of crazy ideas. Don't pay any attention to him.'

She felt she'd already given them too much time and was about to leave. She said with a forced smile, 'I must remember that.'

'Will you be in the lounge later?' Cal asked.

'Why?'

He gave her a knowing look. 'I've got some news for you about that boy friend you haven't been able to find.'

She frowned. 'Are you serious?'

'Yes,' he said. 'I'll see you in the lounge.'

She left him in a state of excitement and fear. She hoped that he really did have some news for her about David Barry and at the same time she feared that he might be just leading her on.

Edna was at the door when she returned. The white-haired woman asked her, 'What was all the talk about? Didn't those two like their table?'

Andrea said, 'They were just making small talk. Nothing to worry about.'

'I'm glad of that,' she said. 'I'm not too fond of them. I've been waiting for them to make some sort of trouble.'

It appeared that Monty Freeman had noticed her lingering at the table as well. He'd been playing in the dining room at the time and when he finished his set of tunes he halted by her on his way out for a break.

'What goes on with Cal Wayne and his friend?' he asked her.

She gave him a nervous smile. 'So you saw me talking there too.'

'I did.'

'He says he has something to tell me about David Barry,' she said.

'Oh?' Monty glanced across the dining room to the table of the two men. 'Better watch out with him. Don't make a date to go anywhere outside the hotel to get the information.'

'I won't,' she promised. 'Do you think he's lying to me?'

'Who knows?'

'That's why I feel I have to give him a

chance to talk to me,' she said. 'I'm to meet him in the lounge.'

Monty looked relieved. 'At least I won't be far away.'

'That's what I considered when I agreed to see him in there,' she said.

Monty went on out and she remained at the door. A little later when Cal Wayne and the jockey left the room, Cal paused to speak to her again.

'Don't forget,' he said.

'I won't,' she promised.

'I'll make it easy for you,' the man with the dark glasses said. 'I'll have a table reserved.'

'There's no need,' she protested.

'Let me arrange it,' he said. And he went on out.

She had to remain in the dining room until it closed and she and Edna went over the receipts. Then she quickly freshened up and made her way across the lobby to the lounge. It was already well-filled and Monty was playing the piano.

She remained in the entrance for a moment and then the head waiter came to her and said, 'Mr. Wayne is at his table waiting for you.'

'Thank you,' she said nervously. And as she went by the piano she gave Monty a quick smile. He nodded back to her gravely and went on playing.

Cal had chosen a table out of sight of the piano. She felt he'd probably done it

97

deliberately, knowing of her interest in Monty. He was alone at the table for two and got to his feet as the waiter pulled out her chair for her.

He said, 'I was beginning to worry that you weren't going to show up.'

Sitting, she said, 'I was kept late in the dining room.'

'Sure,' Cal agreed, sitting again and gazing across the table at her intently. 'Sure. I know how it can be. The main thing is you're here now.'

'Yes,' she said. 'What about David Barry?'

He smiled and lifted a protesting hand. 'Don't rush things. Let's order first.' And he signaled for a waiter.

After he had ordered for them, she said, 'I don't want to annoy you but I'm terribly anxious to hear anything you have to tell me about David Barry.'

There was a cruel expression on the face of the young man with the dark glasses. He said, 'I guess you don't enjoy my company much.'

'It's not that!' she protested. 'But I am concerned about David. What have you found out about him?'

The dark glasses fixed on her. He was silent for a moment so that the music of Monty's piano and the conversation of the others in the room were apparent to her. Then in a hard voice he said, 'I guess what I learned is important. David Barry is dead.'

CHAPTER FIVE

Andrea was stunned by the revelation offered by the man in the dark glasses. It was the last thing she had expected to hear. He seemed so certain about it that she was engulfed by a sickening chill.

'You must have made a mistake!' she gasped.

'Why?'

'I had a phone call from David Barry last night.'

A grim smile played about the lips of the man sitting opposite her in the dark lounge. He said, 'In that case it must have been a call from the dead.'

'Don't talk like that!' she begged him.

'I've told you. David Barry is dead.'

'It isn't possible!' Andrea protested, yet realizing that it could well be. It was just that she didn't want to believe it. All her hopes just couldn't end in this tragic way. Yet she was fairly certain the phone call had been the work of a cruel prankster. Or might it have been that of a ghost?

Cal Wayne was studying her cynically. He said, 'I've used all my contacts and I've found this out for you. Now you refuse to listen to me!'

She stared at him. 'When did it happen?'

'About two weeks ago.'

She knew that fitted in. David Barry had been in Saratoga for more than that time. But she was still reluctant to believe the story. She asked, 'How?'

Cal smiled weakly. 'That's a fairly long story.'

'I want to hear it,' she insisted.

He hesitated, seeming not to want to continue. He made a show of listening to Monty's piano playing for a moment or two before he commented, 'He's good, isn't he?'

'Yes,' she said impatiently. 'But you haven't told me about David Barry!'

The dark glasses fixed on her. 'I think it's enough that you know he's dead. That should settle it. Your next move ought to be to get out of here before the ghost of the silk-stocking murderer or some other phantom tries to kill you.'

She decided he was merely trying to terrify her and get her to leave Saratoga. She said, 'There are other things I'm more afraid of than ghosts.'

'The Ansonia Hotel has a dark history,' he warned. 'You wouldn't be the first young woman to die here mysteriously.'

'Please don't change the subject! Tell me about David Barry!'

'Very well,' he said. 'But you won't be any better off after you hear the story.'

'Let me be the judge of that.'

Cal Wayne rubbed the edge of the table with the fingers of his right hand. It was another nervous gesture showing his reluctance to divulge the facts about David Barry's death. She was beginning to wonder if what he'd told her was true.

He said, 'David Barry made a practice of coming to Saratoga every August. He was a regular at the Saratoga Race Course—one of a group mixed up in a crooked gambling operation in connection with the races.'

'How can you know all that?' she demanded.

He smiled coldly. 'I have friends in the same racket if you must know.'

She said, 'That doesn't surprise me.'

'Thanks.'

'David was a newspaperman. I can't see why he'd get himself involved in a gambling operation.'

'I don't know what he was,' Cal Wayne said. 'But it's not all that strange for newspaper people to join up with gamblers. Their jobs on the papers often mean they get good tips. They are also able to spread false information and sometimes change the betting odds on races.'

She hadn't thought about this and again she was forced to realize that it was all too likely David Barry might have found an alliance with gamblers profitable. He had taken a leave of absence from his paper; perhaps he did this every year during the racing season.

She said, 'Where was he staying?'

'At a motel called The Steeplechase not too far from the race course,' Cal Wayne said with the assurance of one who knew all the facts. 'It's a headquarters for the gambling crowd. Hardly anyone else stays there in season.'

'What happened?'

The man in the dark glasses gave her a knowing look. 'From what I've been able to find out, your friend David pulled a couple of fast ones on the regular crowd. Conned them out of a hefty amount of money. When they told him they didn't like it and wanted a settlement he just laughed at them. That crowd isn't the kind to take being double-crossed and laughed at lightly. A few nights later David Barry had an accident.'

'What sort of accident?' she asked in a strained voice.

'He was having trouble with his car and took it across the highway to a service station to be checked. When he was walking back to the motel around dusk he was run down by a hit-and-run driver. By the time the service station people got to him he was dead.'

'Have they located the hit-and-run car?' she asked.

He shook his head. 'They're not liable to. I understand the police investigation is going on.'

She was shocked by the cold precision of it

all. 'But you don't expect them to bring his killer to justice?'

'I don't think they have a hope.'

'What did they do with the body?'

'He's buried somewhere here in Saratoga,' Cal Wayne said. 'It turned out that he had no relatives in New York but he did have a cousin living here. It also turned out that he had no money. They didn't find any cash in his motel room which wasn't surprising since the boys who lost their money to him likely got there first and looted the place.'

'Would the motel proprietor allow that?' she asked in astonishment.

'Nick Lucas owns the place and he's one of the gambling crowd,' Cal Wayne said with a thin smile. 'There's a kind of sentimental ending to the story. The boys at the motel tossed in enough cash between them to pay for David Barry's funeral costs and a nice headstone. The end!'

'That's horrible!' she gasped.

He shrugged. 'That's the way it goes in that racket.'

'I still think you've made a mistake,' she protested. 'It doesn't sound like the David Barry I knew!'

'How well did you know him?' Cal Wayne asked.

She winced at the sardonic tone of his question. And she knew that he had the best of her. She didn't want to admit to him that their friendship had come about by means of a computer and that she'd never actually met the young man face to face.

She said, 'I thought I knew him very well.'

'It seems you didn't.'

'I don't know,' she said unhappily.

'In any case it's no longer important,' Cal Wayne said. 'David Barry is dead. You need concern yourself no more about him.'

She gave him a look of anguish. 'But only last night he called me. At least the voice on the phone claimed to be David Barry.'

Cal Wayne smiled cynically. 'A ghostly phone call!'

'Don't make light of it!'

'What did this voice sound like?'

'It was strange, muffled, not at all clear.'

'Did it seem anything like David Barry's voice?'

Again she was caught in an awkward spot. She said, 'I can't be sure.'

'You seem to have trouble being sure about anything,' was Cal Wayne's comment.

'It's very confusing!' she protested.

'So I gather,' he said. 'What did this phantom on the phone say to you?'

'Not too much.'

'What?'

In a low voice, she said, 'He told me he didn't want to see me. He asked me to leave here.'

'Interesting!'

She gave him a troubled look. 'What do you make of it?'

Cal Wayne said, 'I'd say some of the gambling crowd have heard through the underground that you're here looking for David Barry. They're worried that you might know too much and want you to get out of town.'

'How would they hear about me?'

He nodded toward the bar. 'When you started those fellows behind the bar asking questions you began something you won't be able to end so easily.'

'I see,' she said.

'Most of the underworld here have heard you're looking for Barry by now,' Cal Wayne went on. 'Your phone call was probably made by one of them.'

'You think so?'

'Yes. And under the circumstances I'd say you'd be wise to follow their advice. It's the same I've given you more than once.'

'They killed David! Why should I allow them to scare me away?'

'For the very good reason they might decide to eliminate you as well,' he said mockingly.

'I'm completely confused,' she lamented. 'I don't know what to do.'

'You might begin by thanking me for getting all this information for you,' he said. 'You don't seem blessed with a grateful nature.'

'I do appreciate what you've done,' she told

him. 'But you'll admit the news wasn't all that good. I'm still in a kind of shock.'

'I'll forgive you on that basis,' he said.

She stared at him. 'All the time I have the feeling you are playing some cat and mouse game with me. That you enjoy taunting me!'

Cal Wayne looked hurt. 'That's very unfair of you.'

'I can't help it. It is how I feel.'

He said, 'I've tried to be a friend to you and you think more of that piano player.'

She blushed at this mention of Monty. 'I don't see how you can get that idea.'

'I know,' the man said.

'I still have found out so little about you,' she protested. 'I don't know what you do. Why you are here.'

He said, 'I thought I explained that to you.'

'You made a lot of silly talk about your business being making friends. It didn't add up.'

'You think not?' the man across the table from her said. 'Well, I'll tell you more plainly. I'm a trainer for one of the stables.'

This sounded logical to her. She said, 'Why didn't you tell me that in the first place?'

'I wanted to test your belief in me.'

'I think you were anxious to keep me in the dark,' she told him. 'What stables employ you?'

He hesitated just a fraction of a moment before he said, 'I'm with the Fred J. Locke

106

stables.'

'Does Slim Gordon jockey for them?'

'Sometimes.'

'And that's why you're friendly with him?'

'We're not all that friendly.'

'You see him sometimes,' she said. 'He comes to dinner with you at the hotel.'

'That's mostly when we meet,' Cal Wayne said. He raised his eyes and gazed beyond her as he added, 'Your friend, Monty, is leaving the piano at this minute. I'm going to go now and leave the field open to him. Otherwise he'll be jealous.'

'Don't be silly!' she protested.

He rose from the table and tossed several bills in the dish left by the waitress. 'That will pay for the check. And don't forget what I've said. Your best bet is to get out of here as soon as you can.' He left with a parting nod before she could make any reply.

Cal had barely vanished in the direction of the bar when Monty Freeman came up by the table with a worried, questioning look on his pleasant face.

'I saw you had a long session with Wayne.'

'Yes. Do sit down,' she pointed to the empty chair.

He sat. 'What did he have to tell you?'

'Something so startling you won't believe it.'

'Try me.'

'David Barry is dead! At least so he says!'

He looked shocked. 'Dead?'

'And buried,' she said grimly.

'But you talked with him on the phone last night. At least that's what you told me.'

'I thought I did.'

'Tell me the whole thing quickly,' the pianist told her. She did. And she ended with, 'If it isn't true, it's an amazing pack of lies.'

Monty looked worried. 'You're right. It sounds authentic.'

'I'll have to think about it.'

The pianist's face was grave. 'If I were in your place I'll tell you what I'd do.'

'What?'

'Follow the advice Cal Wayne and that voice on the phone gave you,' he said. 'I'd leave Saratoga. Something is going on here you'd be lucky to miss. I'm sure of it.'

'You may be right,' she agreed. 'But before I go I want to be sure about David Barry.'

'That could take just long enough to get you in real trouble,' Monty warned her.

She looked at him bleakly. 'You're all so anxious to see the last of me. I thought you cared about me.'

'I do,' her friend said. 'I don't want to see you hurt.'

'I think I can take care of myself.'

Monty gave a deep sigh. 'I don't like anything I've heard. And on top of everything else there's the extra danger you subject yourself to by remaining in this hotel.'

'You mean from the silk-stocking phantom?'

Monty gave her a reproving look. 'Don't talk about it so glibly. You'd be wise to be frightened of it.'

'Don't you think I have enough troubles without that?'

'I think you should remember what has happened to pretty young girls who lived here before and realize it might be your turn next.'

'I doubt it.'

'Why?'

'I have an idea the killings are over. The ghost of that murderer is finally at rest.'

Monty looked grim. 'I wish I could agree. I can't.'

She said, 'You'll have to start playing again in a few minutes and I'm going up to bed. What I've heard tonight has really shocked me.'

'Not enough or you'd be planning to return to New York,' Monty said. 'When I finish my engagement here I could go to the city and meet you.'

'Perhaps we will work out something like that,' she said. 'I don't know yet.' She got up from the table.

He got to his feet as well. 'I'll see you tomorrow,' he said.

'Yes.'

'Think it over and give Clayton your resignation,' Monty said as they parted.

She knew that he meant it and yet she couldn't think of leaving Saratoga until she learned more about the fate of David Barry. Had Cal Wayne deliberately lied to her? She scanned the bar but he was no longer sitting there nor was the jockey, Slim, there either.

Andrea went on out to the lobby. And though it was not as late as the previous night she again found it deserted and nearly dark. The elderly Grant was standing behind his desk and on seeing her he at once called out to her.

'Miss Gibbs!'

She went over to the desk. 'Yes?'

The bald, hollow-cheeked Grant said, 'I've been trying to get you in your room.'

Startled, she asked, 'Oh? Why?'

'Someone has been trying to reach you on the phone.'

She frowned. 'Do you know if it was the same person who called me last night?'

His rheumy blue eyes showed uneasiness as if he might be hedging as he replied, 'I couldn't say. I only know they've called here two or three times in the last hour.'

'Was it a man?'

'Maybe,' the clerk replied warily. 'I don't pay much attention to calls.'

'I see,' she said. 'Well, I'll be in my room for the rest of the night if there should be another call.'

'I'll put it through to you,' Grant rasped.

She left the desk and went across to the elevator. She saw that its gate was open and someone was standing inside its shadowy interior ready to serve as operator. She thought the regular man went off at ten and believed this to be his substitute. The man nodded as she entered the elevator.

'The fourth floor,' she told him. 'I didn't know you helped with the elevator as well,' she said to the man she recognized as Olaf, the night watchman.

The big man closed the elevator door and in his sing-song voice said, 'I do what is needed. I fill in for everyone.'

'So it seems,' she said, as the elevator made a slow, creaking ascent. 'This elevator seems very old and in not too good shape.'

'Like the hotel,' Olaf said gloomily. 'It has seen its best days and so have most of us here.'

She smiled at the giant of a man. 'You look healthy enough.'

'But I am not,' he said. 'My heart is bad.'

'I'm sorry,' she said. 'Have you always lived in this part of the country?'

'Since I came over from the old country,' he said. 'But I have moved around. Always I have come back.'

'You must like it.'

'It has memories for me,' Olaf said as the elevator came to a halt and he opened the gate for her. 'Goodnight, Miss.'

'Goodnight,' she said. 'And thank you.'

He nodded. 'Yes, Miss.' And then he closed the door and she heard the elevator begin its

111

noisy descent.

She moved on in the gloomy corridor to her own room. She passed the door of Edna's room and wondered where she was tonight. She had come to like the pleasant white-haired woman who served as captain in the dining room.

Unlocking the door of her own tiny room she went in and turned on the lights. Then she closed and locked the door after her. The news that she'd been receiving phone calls had shaken her almost as much as the revelation from Cal Wayne that David Barry was dead.

It had put her in a frame of mind where she didn't know what to believe. And Monty Freeman hadn't helped her any with his particular brand of skepticism. Something told her she hadn't heard all the truth from Cal Wayne. The horse trainer had been almost too glib in recounting the story of David Barry's death and what had led up to it.

She felt she just couldn't take his word for it all and give up. She was reasonably sure that she cared for David Barry. At least she'd cared for the man revealed in his letters. And she wasn't going to leave Saratoga without checking more about the fate of the man she might have loved.

It was more difficult to make a decision about Cal Wayne. He had a kind of cold fascination about him. She didn't think he'd deliberately hurt her and yet she felt he enjoyed tampering with her feelings. Trying her to see just how much tension she could take. She knew she feared him a little even though he might be advising her to the best advantage.

As for Monty Freeman, she liked him a great deal. And yet he was an enigma to her. He refused to reveal anything about his past beyond a certain point. So she still knew very little about him. What did worry her concerning him was his obsession with the silk-stocking murders. He had once said he thought the recent murders had not been the work of the ghost of the original killer but had been done by somebody who identified with that long-ago deaf and dumb murderer. She wondered if Monty might be that person.

And then she dismissed the possibility as too unlikely. After all, he was new in town. All this left her back where she'd started. If David Barry was dead who had made the phone call last night? Or the calls tonight? His ghost, perhaps?

She decided to try and cope with most of these questions in the morning. She was weary now and needed her rest. She prepared for bed as quickly as she could and turned out the lights. Once in bed she was again troubled by the things she'd heard during the evening. Her upset mind made sleep difficult.

It was a fairly warm and humid night and she debated about opening the window. She got out of bed and crossed to the window and unlocked the latch, then she raised the sash. There was a rusty screen outside to give some protection against insects. She made sure the sash would stay up by itself.

As she was about to leave the window she glanced down into the yard behind the hotel. And she gave a small start for she was almost certain she saw a solitary figure standing down there in the darkness gazing up at her window. She couldn't make out who it was and after a moment the figure seemed to melt into the shadows. She could see it no more but it had given her a shock.

She returned to her bed and again tried to sleep. But it was not to be easy. She kept turning restlessly and found herself unable to relax. The room seemed dreadfully hot in spite of the open window. She stared up into the darkness and thought about that mystery figure she'd seen in the yard.

Then the phone on the table beside her bed rang sharply. She gave it a frightened look and slowly reached for it with a hand whose trembling betrayed her fears.

'Yes,' she said into the phone.

There was no immediate answer. Just a mocking silence.

'Yes? Who is it?' she demanded.

Then the voice came the same as on the previous night. A harsh, muffled voice and it said, 'You haven't obeyed me!'

Swallowing hard, she replied, 'Tonight I was told that you are dead.'

There was a chuckle from the other end of the line. 'Then listen to what a ghost has to tell you. Leave the Ansonia Hotel and Saratoga! Forget about me!'

'But why?' she protested.

She was protesting to a dead line. Once again the mysterious caller had hung up on her. Distressed she replaced the phone and lay back on her pillow. What did it mean?

This thought was still tormenting her when she finally did sleep. A sleep in which a phantom figure with a skull for a face confronted her and told her he was David Barry. It was a wild, complicated dream and she emerged from it with a small cry of terror.

Then she lay awake there again. And as she did so she was all at once aware of a board creaking at the far end of her bedroom. It made her rise up in bed and she was almost sure she saw a form move stealthily in the shadows.

'No!' she cried out in terror and drew back against the head of the bed.

Her heart was pounding wildly as she stared into the utter darkness of the room. Now all seemed quiet again. The presence of which she'd been so aware seemed to have vanished. Was it the ghost she'd heard so much about whose shadowy presence had entered the room and then left it again? Was the silk-stocking phantom stalking her? The thought sent an icy chill through her!

She wanted to turn on the lights but didn't dare move out of bed. She continued in this state of terror until dawn began to show and she saw that the room was truly empty. Then she slept again. As a result of her restless night she overslept and it was after nine before she awoke.

She hastily washed and dressed and went down for her breakfast. Edna gave her a genial nod of greeting as she entered the dining room. And when she went to the tables reserved for the staff she met the manager on his way out.

Ernest Clayton halted to speak to her. 'You are late this morning.'

'Yes. I didn't sleep well until it was dawn.'

'Insomnia?' the manager asked, with interest showing on his purplish face.

'I suppose you'd call it that.'

'I'm bothered by it myself,' he said sympathetically. 'There are nights when I pace up and down and can't get to sleep. My doctor has given me some tablets which help. But I don't like to become too dependent on them.'

'That can be dangerous,' she agreed.

The stout manager nodded. 'It's not a very satisfactory solution but one has to have sleep.' And he continued on his way out.

She sat down and ordered a light breakfast. The manager was beginning to interest her as

116

a person. In the beginning she'd scarcely given him a thought but now she was beginning to wonder about him. She must ask him about the murders when the opportunity presented itself.

When she finished breakfast she sought out Edna and asked her about the Steeplechase motel. She said, 'Someone told me about it last night.'

Edna gave her a sharply inquiring glance. 'It's not much of a place.'

'I realize that,' she said. 'I just wondered where it is located.'

The white-haired woman said, 'It's not far from the race track. I mean the main track that is used this month for the big races. There is another track used for trotting races that's a distance from there.'

'If you'll tell me the street and the general direction I'm sure I can find it,' she said.

Edna carefully explained how to get to it. Then she said, 'I hope you'll pardon me for asking. But why would you want to go to a place like that? It's where all the gamblers hang out.'

She said, 'I have a newspaper reporter friend who sometimes stays there.'

Edna grimaced. 'Well, I suppose it would be a good place to pick up news.'

Andrea left the gray old hotel and got into her car. She always felt freer and better outside the confines of the ancient building.

There was some strange atmosphere of gloom about the shabby place which bothered her whenever she was in it. Perhaps only in the lounge did she seem to escape it because of the crowds and music there.

Thinking of the music made her wonder where Monty Freeman might be on this fine August morning. He never seemed to show himself around the hotel until later in the day when he reported for work. She assumed he must have a room there but she really didn't know.

Following Edna's instructions she drove through the lovely old city with its huge trees shadowing the streets and made her way to the Steeplechase motel without taking a wrong turn. She drove into the parking area by the front of the motel and turned off the car engine.

The Steeplechase motel was a dark green rambling building with white trim. It was only one story high and consisted of an office area in the center and two wings extending out in wide angles from this central portion. The wings contained about fifteen units each. A neon sign over the center portion announced the name of the place. This blue and red sign apparently remained on all day and night.

A few cars were parked before various sections of the motel and she noted that all of them were expensive and showy in contrast to the seedy appearance of the place itself.

Summoning her courage she got out of her car and walked to the aluminum screendoor which gave entry to the office and went inside. The odor of coffee assailed her nostrils and she saw that the inside of the building had the same run-down look as the outside.

There was a bell mounted on the worn counter which was liberally covered with burns from carelessly discarded cigarettes. Since there was no one in sight she pressed the bell which rang somewhere out back. After a moment a slatternly looking redheaded woman came out a rear doorway and gave Andrea a bored look.

'What is it?' the woman asked in a husky voice.

Remembering the name of the proprietor as told to her by Cal Wayne, she said, 'I'd like to speak with Mr. Lucas.'

'Nick?'

She nodded. 'Yes.'

The woman eyed her doubtfully. 'I don't know whether he has time to see you or not,' she said.

'I wish he would.'

'What do you want to see him about?'

Andrea hesitated, then rather nervously, she said, 'I want to ask him about a friend of mine who has stayed here.'

The slatternly one became wary. 'We don't give out any information about our guests.'

'This is different,' she said quickly. 'It's

about someone who is dead.'

'Dead?'

'Yes. Maybe you knew him. His name was David Barry.'

The stout woman in the faded print dress reacted at once. She took on a nervous look. 'You knew him?'

'Yes. And I wanted to ask Mr. Lucas some questions about his death. I've only just heard about it.'

The woman was staring at her with suspicion. She said, 'Wait a minute.' And she lumbered off through the rear doorway to the back again.

Andrea stood there waiting. While she was there alone the door opened and the jockey, Slim Gordon, stepped inside. He was on his way to the counter when he saw her and a shocked look came to his long, gloomy face. The little man turned and bolted out of the office with the screendoor clanging in his wake. It would have been almost a comic interlude if she hadn't been so tense.

She heard a footstep and turned to see that a short, stout man had entered through the rear door. He wore badly wrinkled dark trousers and an underwear top cut low so that she could see his hairy chest. He was partly bald with black hair heavy at the sides of his head and he had the puffed, purple face of a drinker. He had a flat nose and a broad ugly face with tiny red eyes and at least a two-day growth on his face.

He came rather unsteadily to the counter and growled, 'Who are you?'

'You wouldn't know me,' she said nervously.

The puffed face showed anger. 'You can just bet I wouldn't,' he told her. 'If you got any questions to ask about David Barry why don't you go to the police instead of bothering me?'

'I didn't like to go to the police,' she said, hoping he'd think she had good reasons for this. 'I felt you wouldn't mind helping me.'

'Helping you with what?'

'He spent his last days here, didn't he?'

The squat man continued to stare at her suspiciously. 'He was living here when someone ran him down on the highway.'

'That's what I heard,' she said. 'Did he leave any possessions here? Any letters or a picture of himself?'

'All that stuff was taken by the police,' Nick Lucas told her. 'You take a tip from me you'll forget him. He wasn't no guy for a dame like you. And his name spells trouble in this town.'

'I didn't realize that.'

'Well, I'm telling you now. He's dead and maybe a good riddance. That's all I got to say.'

Seeing that she was quickly approaching a dead end, she said, 'He had some letters. I want them back. They wouldn't mean anything to you or the police. But they are valuable to me.'

'I can't help you,' the surly Nick Lucas said.

'The only one who might be able to would be his cousin. And I doubt if she will since she's a little crazy!'

CHAPTER SIX

Andrea knew she had to find some way to get cooperation from the aggressive, puffy-faced Nick Lucas if she were to learn the truth about David Barry. Ordinarily she would have retreated before his angry comments but too much was at stake in this case. She had to persevere.

She said, 'If you'll give me his cousin's address I'll not bother you again.'

'No?' the squat man seemed far from convinced.

'I promise,' she said. 'This thing I'm concerned about has nothing to do with whatever David Barry came here for. It's a personal thing.'

'You're going to a lot of trouble just the same,' the man in the T-shirt and wrinkled slacks said.

'It's my letters. I said things in them I wouldn't want others to find out about,' she pleaded with him.

Nick Lucas showed disgust. 'Okay. So I'll give you that crazy dame's name and address. But it won't do you any good!'

'I'll risk that.'

'I don't want you comin' here again, get that?' the squat man with the ugly, beard-stubbled face warned her. 'I don't want to ever hear about Barry again!'

'I understand,' she said.

'You'd better,' was his reply. 'This cousin of his lives on Lincoln Street over a drugstore. You can't miss the place; it's the only corner drugstore on the street and she lives on the floor above it. Her name is Bertha Walsh and you're welcome to her.'

'Can I say that you sent me?' she asked.

'It wouldn't make any difference if you did,' he said with an air of disgust.

'Thank you,' she said and turned to leave.

'Remember! Don't come back!' he called after her.

She escaped from the motel office with a feeling of deep relief. There was nothing about Mr. Nick Lucas that she liked. And Cal Wayne's story of how David Barry was framed and kilted after incurring the anger of the gambling ring seemed more reasonable after this brief contact with them.

She drove away from the motel as quickly as possible. She had a vague idea where Lincoln Street was. As she remembered it ran the same way as the main business street but was a block east from it. She made her way to the general business area and began searching for the street.

At last she got her car headed down the somewhat shabby Lincoln Street and after a short distance she saw the drugstore at the corner of an intersection a little ahead. She

124

slowed down the car and found an empty parking meter. Then she walked to the drugstore and found the doorway leading to the apartments above it.

It wasn't a new or well-kept building. The stairs were dark and narrow. A heavy odor of stale cabbage overwhelmed her as she mounted the steep flight to the second floor.

There was just enough light on the landing for her to see the door and the name of Bertha Walsh typed on a card and thumbtacked on it. At least she'd come to the right place. There wasn't a sound from inside as she groped for the doorbell and pressed it.

No one answered the door right away but after a few moments it was opened on a chain. She vaguely saw a feminine figure in a dark blue robe through the crack in the doorway.

A whining female voice inquired, 'What do you want?'

'I'd like to speak to you for a minute, Mrs. Walsh,' she said.

The face on the inside came nearer the narrow opening so that Andrea had a glimpse of a worn face, large blue glasses and a mop of henna-colored hair.

'Did Joe send you?' the woman asked eagerly.

'No.'

Disappointment shadowed the pale, worn face. 'Who, then?'

'I've been talking with Nick Lucas about

your cousin and he sent me here.'

'Nick Lucas! I don't want anything to do with him or anyone connected with him!' the woman cried out in a panic and she tried to close the door.

Andrea quickly put all her weight against it and pleaded, 'Please, listen to me. I'm not a friend of Nick Lucas, I was a close friend of your cousin's.'

'David was a good cousin!' the woman inside said with a sudden sobbing that came as a surprise. Nick Lucas had been right in suggesting she was badly off mentally.

She knew she had to beg hard. It was her only chance. She said, 'I know what a good person David was, and I only want to see you and help you. Just as he did!'

The face peered out at her nervously. 'How can I be sure if you are a friend of Nick Lucas?'

'I'm not,' she protested. 'I just happened to talk to him.'

'Lucas is a killer!' Bertha Walsh said with a new burst of sobbing. 'He had my cousin killed!'

'Let me in. We can talk about that.'

'The police said not to talk to anyone!'

'They were afraid of you betraying yourself to an enemy,' Andrea argued. 'I'm your friend. I was in love with David.'

This seemed to hit some responsive chord in the hysterical woman inside. She stared out into the dark hallway. 'You and my cousin?'

'Yes. We were very interested in each other.'

'I don't believe it!'

'You will if you let me in and give me a hearing,' Andrea pleaded with her.

The woman peering out the crack of the door hesitated. 'I don't know,' she said. 'I don't think so. I'm expecting someone. And I don't want any company when they come.'

'They needn't know I'm there. I'll hide in another room, keep quiet. Do anything you like if you'll just see me!'

Again a hesitation. Bertha Walsh said, 'I can't afford any trouble. You understand?'

'Yes. I'll make you no trouble.'

'If I let you in for a few minutes will you promise not to stay? Joe is sending someone to see me and I have to be alone when he gets here! I have to!'

'I won't stay a moment longer than you want me to,' she promised.

There was another pause from inside and Andrea waited tensely to see if she'd convinced the weird Bertha. Then after a long moment the chain was removed from the door and it was opened for her to enter.

The first thing that struck her about the tiny apartment was its squalor and shabbiness. Things were strewn on chairs and tables about the small living room as if it hadn't been tidied up in months. And it probably hadn't! But it was Bertha Walsh herself who caught her attention most.

Bertha was a thin, short woman with henna-colored hair frizzed lamely. Perhaps she'd once been pretty but now her face was pale and pinched. Her blue eyes behind the large pale-blue glasses continually showed a wild-eyed expression of fear. She wore a flowing blue housecoat and held her hands tensely before her. And she at once gave a hint of her taut state by a gesture she used continually. To emphasize any point she beat the air with her forearms in rhythmic fashion.

'What do you want from me?' Bertha asked.

Somewhat disconcerted Andrea said, 'I want to ask you a few things about your cousin, David. Did the police return any letters of his to you?'

'No,' the thin woman said in a frightened voice. 'They haven't given me anything of his. And those crooks took all David's money. He used to give me money! Since he was killed I've had nothing!' The sob came back to her throat again.

Andrea reached in her pocketbook and brought out a twenty dollar bill and handed it to the woman. 'Perhaps that will be a little help.'

'Thank you,' Bertha said and snatched the bill greedily in a scrawny hand and stuffed it in a pocket of her housecoat.

'I wrote David some letters. I'd like to get them back.'

128

Bertha shook her head. 'I don't know anything about them.'

'Did David ever mention me to you? My name is Andrea Gibbs.'

'No,' the pale woman said. 'He didn't talk to me much about his personal affairs. But he came to see me whenever he was here and he was good to me!'

'Why did he leave New York and come to Saratoga?' she asked.

'He always did that.'

'I see,' she said. 'Did he ever give you any suggestion that his life might be in danger?'

'Yes!' Bertha Walsh declared. 'He knew toward the end that gang were out to get him.'

'Why didn't he leave the motel? Even get out of Saratoga?'

'He was too deep in it!' Bertha said, the eyes behind the glasses tragically fixed on her. 'Is that all? You have to leave!'

'Will you try and find out about the letters? Ask the police if you can have them?'

The pale woman with the henna hair nodded. 'I will! I will!'

'I'll be in touch with you again,' Andrea said.

The woman seemed to have a sudden thought. She said, 'For another twenty I'll give you a photo of David. One I've treasured.'

Andrea didn't argue. She dug in her purse for a second twenty dollar bill. Before she could pass it to the nervous woman in blue the skinny hand grasped it from her again.

'I'll get the photo,' the woman mumbled and turned and hurried off into the next room.

Andrea gazed around her at the cheap furniture and the generally drab condition of the apartment. There had to be something wrong with Bertha Walsh for her to live the way she was doing. She wasn't all that old and apart from her nervous state and being so thin she seemed well enough.

The woman with the henna hair returned clutching a framed small-sized photo to her with both hands. 'I have it! I'm only giving it to you because you liked David. And now you have to go!' The woman thrust the photo at her.

She felt a surge of excitement at this opportunity to gaze at the face of her correspondent for the first time. At last she was to have a look at David Barry! She took the photo from the thin woman and stared at it. And at once her feelings of excitement turned to despair. The face she was studying was that of a man of at least fifty with a shifty expression. His age alone indicated it could not be the David Barry she'd had correspondence with.

In a voice filled with disappointment she exclaimed, 'It's a mistake! That's not the same David Barry! Not the man I wrote those letters to!'

Bertha beat the air with her forearms. 'You

told me that it was my David! I didn't try to deceive you!'

'I know,' Andrea said miserably. 'It's all right. Not your fault. You can keep the money. And you may as well have the photo back.'

The woman took the photo and the eyes behind the blue glasses studied it fondly. 'I didn't want to part with it! He was the only one who cared about me!'

'I'm sorry I intruded on you,' Andrea said, feeling almost physically ill that her search for David Barry should have turned out this way.

'It doesn't matter,' the thin woman said with fear in her eyes. 'Just so long as you go before anyone else gets here!'

'I'll go!' She started for the door, anxious to get out of the place.

'Miss!' The woman followed her and called out in a pleading voice. 'Wait, Miss!'

At the door she turned, 'Yes?'

The thin woman was close to her now. 'Let me have your name and address. I might find something out and be able to help you.'

Andrea was hesitant and suspicious of the woman's sincerity. 'I doubt it.'

'David had friends as well as enemies,' Bertha Walsh hastened to say. 'I can talk to some of them and maybe they'll know about this other David Barry.'

She felt it was a waste of time but she decided to take a chance anyway. She said, 'My name is Andrea Gibbs and I'm staying at the Ansonia Hotel.'

'At the Ansonia!' Bertha nodded. 'I'll remember. Andrea Gibbs!'

'That's right,' she said wearily and stepped out on the landing.

The thin woman pounded the air with her forearms. 'You'll be willing to pay if I find out anything?'

'Yes,' she said. 'I'll pay. But the information will have to be about my David Barry.'

'I know,' the pale Bertha said nervously. 'Please leave now. He'll soon be coming!'

Andrea started warily down the narrow, dark stairway to the street again and heard the door slam behind her. Why was the thin woman with the blue glasses so strange? Who was the Joe whom she was expecting to send a messenger? What was the weird truth behind the nightmare existence of the thin, aging woman in the blue housecoat?

When she reached the sidewalk she drew in a breath of fresh air with satisfaction. It was good to be out in the clean air and sunshine once more. She made her way back to her car with most of her enthusiasm gone. She felt if she heard from the distraught Bertha again it would be only for the woman with the henna hair to cadge her for money. The interview had cost forty dollars without any results.

Getting into the car she drove back toward the Ansonia. It was close to noon and she would soon have to report for duty. Someone had either deliberately or by accident sent her on a wild goose chase. And Cal Wayne had lied to her in telling her that the David Barry she'd written to was dead. It may either have been a normal mistake or he'd taken advantage of the fact that a David Barry had been killed in Saratoga. At any event she meant to challenge him about it.

As she drove on she did feel better about the fact that the David she'd written to was still alive! Her spirits rose and she realized that she'd never actually accepted that he was dead. It had seemed too unlikely.

There had been a few minutes as she'd listened to Nick Lucas that she'd believed it. Now she could exult in the knowledge that somewhere in this strange city of towering elms and horseracing the David Barry she knew still moved about.

Ahead the Ansonia Hotel's drab outline was etched against the sky. She drove into the parking area and left her car. Then she hurried up to the fourth floor and washed and dressed. As she came out of her room to get the elevator she met Olaf coming along the hall with a kit of tools in one hand.

She smiled at him. 'You never seem to rest,' she said. The big man nodded in solemn agreement. 'Always something.'

'I'm due in the dining room.'

He stared at her strangely. 'You have decided to stay here? You do not mind the

133

place?'

'Not all that much,' she said. 'And I have friends like you to bolster my courage.'

He shook his head. 'I would not want my daughter here.' And he moved on down the hall.

She went to the elevator and rang the bell. She thought what a strange person he was as she watched his huge, slightly bent figure vanish in the shadows.

When the elevator arrived the sour little man known as Mike was on it. He gave her a glare. 'We don't have to service the fourth floor,' he informed her. 'Staff is supposed to use the stairs.'

She got in with him. 'No one told me that. And I've met most of the staff in the elevators.'

The little man at the controls said, 'They're breaking the rules.'

She smiled at him. 'Don't most people do that?'

The sour Mike avoided looking at her. 'I'm just telling you what is right. You can do what you like. That's what most of them around here do anyway.'

'I won't bother you too much,' she promised.

'Makes no difference to me,' Mike said as he opened the door for her at the ground floor.

When she reached the dining room she told

Edna about the episode at the first free moment they had together. The white-haired woman looked indignant at the report.

'Mike gets more impossible every year,' she said. 'I don't know why they keep him on.'

'I don't want Mr. Clayton to hear about it,' Andrea said at once. 'I wouldn't like to see Mike lose his job.'

'Don't worry about it,' Edna said. 'If he gets let out he well deserves it. He's just as complaining with the guests. And by the way, we have two new ones. A Mr. Al Moroni and his friend, Jake Gotell. They're sitting at the table for three over there. They're expecting a third member. Did you ever see such faces? Gangsters if I know anything about people. The crowd these races draw!'

Andrea followed the older woman's glance to study the table in question and saw a dark man with slicked-back black hair, receding at the temples, and a pinched face. He wore a flashy checked suit and flamboyant red tie. At his side was a chunky man of lighter complexion with the battered face of a prizefighter and a drooping left eyelid.

She murmured to Edna, 'Not exactly class patronage.'

'It's what we get these days,' the little woman in the white uniform said as she left to look after some of the geriatrics at their tables.

Andrea remained in the doorway of the dining room. She hadn't been there more than

135

two or three minutes when a black-haired girl, of striking Latin-type beauty, wearing a black slit skirt and a very low-cut red blouse, came to be seated. The girl had a hint of lower class about her which the large diamonds on the fingers of both hands did nothing to alleviate.

She addressed Andrea in a brash way. 'I'm looking for Al Moroni!'

Andrea smiled at her. 'I'll take you to his table.'

The black-haired girl took in the dining room with a disgusted glance. 'This place reminds me of a funeral parlor! How did Al find it?'

Andrea paid no attention to the comment but led the girl to the table with the two newcomers. The man with the oily black hair rose at once to smile and kiss the girl on the cheek. 'Good to see you, Rose!' He indicated his companion. 'You know Jake.'

Rose nodded to the battered-faced man who had made no attempt to rise and greet her. Sitting with the one called Al, she said, 'What a dump! You should see my room!'

Al waved a placating hand at her. 'We got good reasons for being here,' he said. Andrea left the pretty black-haired girl a menu and walked away. She wondered what kind of crooked game had brought this striking trio to Saratoga.

She went back to her station at the door. The elderly guests who always came in to their meals early had all finished eating and were on their way out of the dining room. Many of them nodded to her in friendly fashion. She found herself beginning to warm to these forlorn relics of another age who clung to the ancient hotel which had once been stylish and modern.

While she was waiting for the last of the luncheon guests to finish Monty Freeman came by. He was in sports clothes as usual. He halted to speak to her.

'I tried to phone you this morning but no one answered,' he said.

'I was out.'

'Scouting the town?'

'Something like that.'

'Anything new?'

She smiled wanly. 'I have some things to tell you. I'll be finished here in a few minutes. Perhaps we can meet on the verandah then.'

'Fine,' the young musician smiled at her. 'I'm going in to look over some of my music. It's been getting in a mess.'

He left her and went into the dining room to stand by the piano and sort out music he had there. It took him a little while and as he worked she noticed that the dark girl with the two gangster types had suddenly begun staring at him and now she was mentioning him to the two men. They were all staring at Monty!

The pianist came back to her after a few minutes and said, 'That's done. I'll be out on the rear verandah.'

She nodded. 'Anyplace but by the shuffleboard. I get the creeps there.'

'Better watch out. That could mean something,' he warned.

'A premonition you mean?' she said.

'Something like that.'

'I'd say it was just because I know a girl was the victim of the silk-stocking murderer out there.'

'That would be enough to make you nervous,' he agreed.

She saw the trio headed by Al Moroni leaving their table to exit from the dining room. And in a low voice, she asked him, 'Do they look familiar to you?'

Monty stared at the advancing group with an expression of concern on his pleasant face. He said sotto voice, 'Don't know.'

Al Moroni came out first with Rose trailing behind him and the squat Jake in the rear. As Al Moroni came up to Monty he halted and stared at him.

'Haven't I seen you before?' he asked.

Monty took it casually. 'Maybe.'

'Yeah, I think I have,' Al Moroni said. He turned to the girl. 'You were right, Rose.'

'Sure, we've seen him before,' the black-haired beauty agreed.

Al Moroni addressed himself to Monty again. 'Where did we see you?'

'Hard to say,' Monty told him. 'I've played

piano in a lot of places.'

Moroni smiled grimly. 'Yeah, I guess so. Well, give me a little time and I'll remember.' And with that the trio went on out into the lobby.

Andrea gave the young man a nervous smile. 'Well, how do you like our latest guests?'

'We could do better.'

'I agree,' she said. 'They seem to think they know you.'

Monty looked unhappy. 'They've probably seen me in some New York spot.'

'You've never told me where you played in the city,' she said.

'I'll get around to it,' he said evasively. 'I'll see you on the verandah.'

'Yes. In a little while,' she told him.

She watched him cross the lobby and carefully avoid the trio led by Al Moroni. And once again she had some doubts about him. From the start he'd behaved in a mysterious way and he hadn't really told her as much about himself as Cal Wayne had. At least she knew Cal was a trainer. But she had no idea what Monty's background was aside from the fact he was a professional pianist.

There had been some kind of recognition between the trio and Monty. She had no idea whether they were trying to cover up something or not. She knew that Al Moroni and his companions had come to the Ansonia

Hotel for a purpose. Could the purpose have anything to do with Monty? Or the mystery of the vanished David Barry?

Once again she began to question whether Monty might be David Barry. It wasn't beyond possibility. He'd only recently arrived in Saratoga and David Barry couldn't have been in the city long. He was making a mystery about his past as David Barry would have to do if he were masquerading as someone else. It was a strange situation. She'd been drawn to Monty as a person in much the same way that the letters from David Barry had convinced her that she would like him. But how could she force Monty to reveal his background?

Edna came over to shut the doors leading into the dining room and check the receipts with her. The white-haired woman said, 'I think I'll go to the races this afternoon.'

She smiled at her. 'I didn't know you were a race fan.'

'Not much point in being in Saratoga if you don't go to the horse races,' Edna said. 'Have you been yet?'

'No.'

'You should go. It's fun and the air does you good. Come along with me if you like.'

'When are you leaving?' Andrea asked.

'I won't be going before three-thirty and I always make sure to get back by five-thirty in time to be down here at six,' Edna said. 'I don't see all the races but I see enough to enjoy them.'

'I'd like to go,' she said. 'I'll be ready at three-thirty and we can use my car.'

'I'll take mine if you like,' Edna said. 'It's not new or stylish but it will get us there. And I do know the shortest way.'

She laughed. 'All right. I think the change might do me good.' She was also thinking that she might keep an eye open for Cal Wayne, since the trainer might very well be at the track.

She and Edna made quick work of going over the checks. Then she was free to meet Monty on the verandah. The young man was seated on a railing near the door. She went out to him.

'I only have a few minutes,' she said. 'I'm going to the races with Edna.'

He looked hurt. 'Why not with me?'

'She works with me and it seemed a fun idea to go with her,' she said.

Monty said, 'You won't be able to stay long.'

'No,' she said, moving to be in the sunshine. 'We just plan to be there a couple of hours.'

The young pianist gave her a questioning look. 'What about this morning?'

'I went in search of information about David Barry,' she said.

'And?'

'I called at the Steeplechase motel and saw Nick Lucas. He told me very little.'

'That figures.'

'And he sent me on to a cousin of David Barry's, a poor unfortunate called Bertha Walsh.'

'Did she help?'

'Yes. Though she didn't mean to,' Andrea said with a wry smile. 'She showed me a photo of David Barry, her cousin. And it wasn't the David I'm looking for at all. This man was much too old. Cal Wayne told me about the wrong man. Probably he did it by accident but I wonder.'

Monty's eyebrows raised. 'So David Barry isn't dead after all.'

'No.'

'Then I have another rival again,' the pianist said with a bleak look.

'Is that all you get out of my news?' she asked him. 'I feel differently about the whole thing. If David had been dead and mixed up in criminal activities it would have soured my being here.'

'Now?'

'Now I'll begin looking for him all over again,' she said.

'Do you honestly expect to find him?'

'Yes.'

'You're an optimist,' the young musician said.

'Have you decided where Al Moroni and his friends met you?' she questioned him. 'You've had time to think it over.'

'No,' he said, looking uneasy. He glanced at

his watch. 'You'd better get on to the races if you're going. You haven't all that much time.'

She noted his desire to stop her questioning him and be rid of her. But she also knew that it was time for her to be on her way.

'I'll see you later then,' she told him and hurried off to meet Edna.

*   *   *

Her first experience of the races was more exciting than she had expected. It was a fine day and the stands were crowded. She and Edna found seats high in the very rear and watched the fast horses as they raced around the track. She was engulfed in a sea of strangers and the hope of finding a familiar face waned.

So she gave all her attention to the various racing events. And she noted that Slim Gordon was riding a horse in one of them. It was number five and with the help of Edna she identified the horse and jockey. The colors were yellow and so it was easy to follow his progress on the track.

It turned out to be a bad race for Slim Gordon. Number five finished far in the rear. Andrea wondered if the little man had been having a series of losing races.

She said to Edna, 'That Slim Gordon sometimes comes to the hotel with Cal Wayne.'

143

'I know,' the white-haired woman said. 'He used to be a famous jockey but he's not had many winning horses in the last few years.'

They remained for another race and then it was time to leave. As they made their way down the numerous steps to the bottom of the grandstand she kept her eyes open for someone she might know but saw no one. They drove back to the hotel and she had time to shower and dress and be at her usual stand by six o'clock. All in all it had been an exciting day.

The dinner crowd was larger than usual which meant she was kept busy. But she was not too busy to note Al Moroni, Jake and Rose when they entered the room. Rose had changed to a long black gown which was too elegant for the dining room on a week-day night and only made the crudity of her companions more noticeable.

Andrea was watching for Cal Wayne but he did not show up for dinner. Neither did Slim Gordon. When the dinner hour ended she and Edna went through the usual business of checking the receipts. Afterward Andrea moved on to the lounge where Monty was already playing. It had become her nightly custom.

She smiled at Monty as she passed and took a table near the piano. And when he finished playing he came over and sat with her.

'How were the races?' he asked.

'I enjoyed them,' she said. 'I didn't see many people I knew. Slim Gordon had a horse in one event.'

Monty's pleasant face showed a wry look of amusement. 'It wasn't a horse from Fred J. Locke's stables was it?'

'I don't know. Why?'

'That's the stable Cal told you he worked for, isn't it?'

She considered. 'Yes, it is. It may have been a horse from that stable Slim was riding.'

'I think not,' Monty said with meaning.

'Why?'

Monty's eyes met hers. 'Because I've done some investigating too. And there is no such stable in Saratoga. Cal Wayne was putting you on.'

She heard the pianist's words with a sense of pain. In spite of everything she had liked Cal Wayne. Now it seemed he had lied to her. He had claimed to be a trainer when he wasn't.

She said, 'That does upset me.'

'He also lied to you about Barry being dead.'

'I know that, but that at least could have been a mistake,' she said. She sighed. 'And he didn't turn up in the dining room tonight.'

'Not likely after all those lies,' Monty said.

She stayed in the lounge for quite a while. Monty played several sets. And then she began to feel tired. She got up from her table and waved to Monty who was still playing and left

145

the lounge.

There was no one to operate the elevator but Grant. After much grumbling, the night clerk left his desk and took her up. She then went to her room and changed into her nightgown and robe. After that she made the journey down the shadowed hall to the bathroom to wash up before going to bed.

She was in a strange troubled mood. And when she reached her room again and opened the door she had an odd sensation of fear. A single light hung from the ceiling giving the room a murky yellow glow. She went on inside and closed the door. She crossed to her bedside and removed her robe and was about to go back and turn off the light by the wall switch.

But as she decided to do this she heard a movement behind her and a heavy breathing. Before she could scream out or even turn to see who it was, something was slipped over her head and tightened around her throat. Her face took on a look of horror and her eyes dilated as she stumbled back with the noose tightening, and realized she was to become another victim of the silk-stocking killer!

CHAPTER SEVEN

Sheer desperation made Andrea cling to consciousness and struggle against the band so surely tightening around her throat. She kept struggling long after it made sense. She heard heavy breathing from above her as her attacker fought to keep the stocking taut around her neck and control her wild efforts to escape.

Then there was a knock on the door of her room and faintly she heard Edna call to her, 'Andrea! May I see you for a moment?'

She tried to shout back and ask for help but no words escaped her tortured lips. She heard Edna pound on the door again and call her name out more loudly. It gave her just a gleam of hope. She felt that Edna knew she was in the room and was now alarmed that she hadn't answered. It seemed to her the pressure was easing slightly on her neck and then she lost consciousness.

When she opened her eyes she was stretched out on the floor of her bedroom and a troubled Edna was bending over her. Her throat ached as if it were on fire.

Edna asked her, 'Who was it?'

Summoning all her strength she said huskily, 'I don't know!'

'When you didn't answer me I knew

something was wrong,' the white-haired woman said. 'So I opened the door and came in. I was just in time to see someone leave by the window. But I couldn't tell who.'

'The ghost!' she said in a hoarse whisper.

The little woman looked blank. 'The ghost?'

'Yes. The ghost of the silk-stocking murderer. He tried to throttle me with a stocking. If you hadn't arrived I would have been murdered.'

Edna looked skeptical. 'I saw a shadowy figure leaving by the window. Whoever it was had almost vanished by the time I got into the room.'

'It must have been the ghost,' she insisted, her brain still in a whirl.

'Didn't you get a look at him either?'

'No,' Andrea said. 'It all happened too quickly. When I came into the room I sensed there was someone in here. Then I was attacked. I never did get a look at my attacker.'

'Then it could have been anyone?'

'I suppose so,' she said wearily, lifting herself up from the floor a little.

Edna was plainly concerned. She said, 'How are you?'

She touched a hand to her throat. 'My throat hurts! It was burned by the silk stocking.'

'You're sure it was a silk stocking?'

'Yes.'

Edna seemed upset by this. 'It's very strange! Just like the other murders that took place here. I'll never feel safe in my bed again.'

'Nor will I,' she said. 'Not as long as I'm in this room.'

The white-haired woman was all sympathy. 'I can understand that, dear. But you mustn't panic,' she advised.

Andrea was weakly sitting up now. 'How did whoever it was get in here?'

'The same way he went out. By that window,' Edna said, nodding toward the opened window. 'There are iron ladders down the sides of the building at several points on this floor. It's supposed to make us safer since the ladders go down to regular iron fire escapes. But I, for one, know I couldn't manage them.'

'Yet my attacker did,' Andrea said forlornly. Her throat had ceased its aching just a little.

Edna said, 'Do you feel able to get up and rest on the bed?'

'Of course,' she said. 'I'm still in a kind of daze. I'm not thinking straight.' And she struggled up from the floor surprised at her weakness. Then she sat on the edge of her bed.

Edna stood there with an air of concern and said, 'I'm going to call Mr. Clayton and tell him what has happened.'

'Please! Should we disturb him at this hour?'

'It's not all that late and he has to know,'

Edna said sternly. With that she picked up the phone.

Andrea sat there miserably and listened to Edna's attempts to locate the manager and give him the message. It took quite a few minutes but the older woman finally managed it. She spoke with Mr. Clayton for a short time, telling him briefly what had happened. Then she put the phone down with a look of grim satisfaction.

The white-haired woman informed her, 'He didn't want to believe it, at first. I had to tell him that I saw someone leaving the room with my own eyes. He's on his way up.'

'That won't do any good,' Andrea protested.

'It should,' Edna said indignantly. 'He has the responsibility to investigate what went on here. If I hadn't come by your door to borrow some thread and a needle you probably would have been murdered.'

'I can't bear to think about it!'

'The fact must be faced.'

'I had no warning,' she said. 'I left the lounge with Monty still playing. Then I came directly up here to go to bed. And it happened!'

Edna's thin face was troubled. She left her and went over to the open window and looked out. Then she drew her head back inside the room and turning to Andrea said, 'It's just as I told you. There's a ladder attached to the building just a couple of feet from the window.

Any agile person could make it down to the fire escape on the next floor, or use it to get up here.'

'I never even thought about it,' she admitted.

The white-haired woman came slowly across the room by the bed again. 'I was here when those other two murders took place. We weren't prepared for them either. I felt there would be no more of them. But it seems I was wrong.'

'They were both done in the same manner as the first silk-stocking killing,' Andrea said.

'Yes,' the thin woman said. 'And the reporters dug up the old murder and manufactured that ghost story. I don't think these recent murders were the work of any ghost. They were done by some madman. I'd hoped that whoever he was must have moved on somewhere. But now it seems that he hasn't.'

She stared at the standing figure of the little woman gloomily. 'Who could it be?'

'Someone connected with the racing season,' Edna said promptly. 'All the killings have taken place during the peak August period.'

'I hadn't realized that.'

'So it is probably someone associated with the racing stables or at least a regular follower of the races.'

Their discussion was interrupted by the

arrival of the manager, Ernest Clayton, with Monty Freeman at his side. The stout manager's florid face wore a look of alarm. The young pianist seemed pale and upset as well.

The manager took charge of the situation, coming to Andrea and asked her, 'Were you actually attacked in this room?'

'Yes,' she said.

'By someone who tried to throttle you with a silk stocking?' he demanded.

'I'm sure that's what it was,' she said. 'It happened very quickly.'

Ernest Clayton looked dumbfounded. 'It's shocking! So we have some mad killer to deal with again!'

Monty Freeman came over beside Andrea and spoke for the first time. His tone was worried. 'I saw you leaving the lounge. When I had my break I started up here. Then I decided you'd probably gone to bed and I'd only bother you. I should have followed through on my first impulse and checked to see that you were all right.'

She said, 'It's not your fault.'

'You could have been killed,' Monty said in a choked voice.

'I just happened to come by her door,' Edna said. 'Now I'm so glad I did.'

Ernest Clayton had left them to look out the open window and inspect the ladder. Now he came back to the middle of the room. 'No secret how the intruder got in here. This old place is impossible to make safe. The locks are old fashioned and can be opened by almost any master key and the windows can't be fastened properly. But I can see that you are put in a different room where there is no handy fire ladder.'

'Thanks,' she said. 'I would appreciate that.'

Edna looked angry. The little woman said, 'We get such an awful class of people these days the criminal is likely one of our own guests!'

The stout Ernest Clayton glared at her. 'Things are bad enough without you suggesting something like that!'

'It's the truth!' the little woman said defiantly.

Monty gave the manager a questioning glance. 'What about the police?'

The manager hesitated. Then he smoothed a hand over his bald head nervously. 'I don't know! We really haven't anything to go on to make a complaint to them.'

Edna said, 'We have an open window and a girl who was nearly strangled by someone.'

Ernest Clayton gave her a despairing glance. 'What I meant to say is that they haven't done anything about the two murders that did take place and they had a lot more evidence to work on. What can we expect this time? And I hate to think what the notoriety will do for the hotel! A good many of our respected older people may consider it the last straw and decide to leave.'

The white-haired woman asked, 'Is that more important than the safety of your employees?'

'I want to do what is best for all concerned,' the stout man said, wringing his hands in a nervous gesture. 'My immediate thought is that we take precautions to guard Miss Gibbs and wait and see if anything more happens. I could have Olaf give more attention to watching this floor at night.'

Monty Freeman was frowning. 'It means taking a certain risk.'

The manager worried, 'The season is at its peak. If we have this story break now in the press it will surely hurt us. I know what happened the last couple of times and a third scare story will make it even worse.'

Andrea felt she should speak up. She said, 'If you feel it is wise not to call in the police yet, I'm willing to go along with it. Just change my room.'

Monty glanced at her. 'You're sure about that?'

'Yes,' she said. She was influenced by the fact that a lot of publicity concerning the attack on her might well mean she'd have to give up her search for the elusive David Barry. Her whole reason for coming to Saratoga would be in jeopardy.

The manager eyed her with relief. 'That is

most considerate of you, Miss Gibbs. And may I say that I think it an intelligent decision as well.'

Edna looked wary of the idea. 'Aren't you afraid?'

'Yes,' she said. 'But I'll be more careful. And I doubt if there'll be another attack on me.'

'I agree,' Clayton said. 'I'll see about another room for you and instruct Olaf to visit this floor more often on his night rounds.'

Andrea said, 'Olaf has so much to do as it is. Is it worth bothering him about this?'

'Definitely,' the manager said. 'He is the night watchman. I'll relieve him of any other duties that interfere with that.'

The next half-hour was a period of flurry. With Edna's aid she gathered up her belongings and they all helped transfer them to another room at the other side of the building closer to the elevator. It was an equally tiny and plainly furnished room but there was no ladder on the outside by its window.

When she was safely installed in the room they all left her. The manager and Edna were the first to leave. Monty remained a moment or two longer to say his goodnight.

Standing in the doorway of her room he studied her with troubled eyes. 'I'm not sure this is the best solution to what happened.'

'It will do for now.'

'I'll worry about you.'

She smiled. 'I know.'

'I still hate myself for not coming all the way up to you,' he went on. 'I took the stairway and was on the second landing when I changed my mind.'

'It's over now.'

'Lock your door and leave the window latched.'

'I intend to.'

'Goodnight,' Monty said. And he took her in his arms for a goodnight kiss. As he let her go, he said, 'I don't know what I'd have done if anything had happened to you.'

'Don't think about it,' she said.

He nodded solemnly and then turned and vanished down the shadowed hall. She closed and locked the door. This new room had the same single cord light descending from the ceiling with its bulb giving off a murky yellowish glow. She gave a tiny shudder as she recalled all the events of the night.

Getting into bed she wondered whether she'd had an encounter with a ghost or some mad human. She certainly couldn't say. Any story she could offer the police would be such a muddled one it wouldn't help. The manager had probably been right in not wanting to go to the authorities on the basis of what had happened.

As she lay in bed staring up into the darkness of the tiny room and seeking sleep she found the image of Cal Wayne forming in her mind. It seemed to her that her attacker could well be the mysterious man with the dark glasses. Edna believed the mad killer was someone who followed the races and came to Saratoga every year. Cal Wayne probably fitted that description. And he had behaved very oddly toward her.

Further, he had not shown himself around the hotel for the past twenty-four hours. If he did return she would know better than to trust him. And at the first opportunity she would discuss him with Ernest Clayton as being the chief suspect.

She finally fell into an exhausted sleep that lasted until it was nearly time to report for work at noon. She quickly got up and washed and dressed. An angry red pattern around her throat was the physical sign of the attack she'd experienced the previous night. A careful coating of cream and powder took care of the skin burn.

Edna greeted her at the entrance to the dining room with a troubled glance. 'I didn't know whether you'd be able to come down or not.'

'I'm all right,' she said, picking up her menus from the table there.

'I still think the police should have been called.'

'Later, perhaps.'

'Later could be too late!' her friend warned.

They had a busy spell when most of the guests arrived. Those interested in the big races came early for lunch. Among this group were the slick-haired Al Moroni, his henchman, Jake Gotell, and Rose. The three were discussing the races among themselves in an animated fashion and hardly paid any attention to Andrea as she showed them to their table.

After the rush, she suddenly felt weary and sat down in a chair near the table in the entry to the dining room. Edna at once noticed and came up to her.

The older woman said, 'You look ill. You don't have to stay any longer. I can manage alone.'

'I feel exhausted.'

'No wonder. Go along. I don't need you. All the people are in,' Edna said.

She got up. 'Thanks. I will accept your offer. I'll go down back and have some soup and crackers. Then I'll try and rest for tonight.'

'Don't come in tonight unless you feel up to it,' Edna told her.

'I'll be all right,' she promised.

She went to the staff table in the rear of the big dining room and had soup. Monty Freeman was still at the piano. He didn't play as long at noon as in the evenings but he was always there. She was about to leave when he came down the room to join her.

Sitting by her, he asked, 'How are you

158

today?'

'Not the best. But I'm coming along.'

The young pianist seemed worried about her. 'You ought to have taken the day off. Clayton would have given it to you. He'll jump any way you like to have you keep quiet.'

She smiled wanly. 'You think so?'

'I know it. He's so afraid of the reputation of his precious hotel.'

'I didn't think calling in the police would help.'

'I'm not sure about it.'

'If there is any more trouble I wouldn't hesitate,' she added.

'Hardly.'

She said, 'No sign of Cal Wayne or that jockey.'

He showed interest. 'You're right. Come to think of it I didn't see either of them in the lounge last night either.'

'I wonder why.'

'Your guess is as good as mine,' the young pianist said. Then their eyes met and he went on, 'You don't think it was Cal last night?'

'I'm wondering.'

'You could be right,' he said excitedly.

'Don't let's be too sure,' she warned him. 'We don't want to start accusing innocent people. He may have nothing to do with it.'

'He's a suspicious character as far as I'm concerned,' Monty commented.

She gave him a look of grim amusement.

'You know it may have been the ghost of the original killer after all.'

'Don't start that!' he declared. 'More likely to be Cal Wayne or maybe that David Barry you're looking for. The way he's acted how do you know he isn't mad?'

'I don't like to mix him up in this,' she protested.

'I think he should be considered,' was his reply. 'You ought to talk to Clayton about him.'

'Later.'

Monty grimaced. 'With you, everything is later. You worry me.'

'I'll handle it my own way,' she promised. And she meant to.

They left the dining room together and parted in the lobby. She went upstairs in the creaking old elevator with Mike at the controls. The little man gave her a sour look.

He said, 'They've made Olaf night watchman, full time. Now I've had to take on a lot of his work.'

She wondered if he knew the reason for the change. And she said, 'Do you really mind so much?'

'They heap work onto me,' the disgruntled Mike said. 'This is my last season here. I'm going on social security.'

'You think you'll be content with that?'

'I ain't content on this job,' he said with annoyance. 'I couldn't do worse.'

'I'm sorry,' she said. She got off at the fourth floor and went to her room to nap. But she found that she couldn't. She was too nervous. So she decided to go for a short walk in the open air and sunshine. That way she might straighten out her thoughts.

She put on a cool linen dress and made her way back to the lobby. She took the stairs down not wanting to confront the irate Mike so soon again in the elevator. Reaching the lobby she nodded and smiled at two of the lady guests who were watching her with interest. They returned the smiles as she moved on to the front door and down the steps to the concrete sidewalk leading to the street.

It was another warm afternoon and she had no definite thoughts as to where she would go. So she started walking slowly toward the parking lot. She'd not gone more than a dozen steps when she heard a horn honk beside her and she turned to see a white hardtop sedan following her slowly at the curb. She halted and glanced in through green tinted windows to see Cal Wayne behind the wheel.

He stopped the car and leaned over as the electric window came down. He said, 'You've saved me a lot of time. I was going into the hotel to look for you.'

She stood warily at the curb. 'Were you?'

'Yes. I want to talk to you. Get in the car before I lose all benefit of the air-conditioning.'

She got in the car. She was worried that she might be making a mistake but still she got in. She closed the door as he rolled the electric window up with the button control beside him.

She said, 'You travel in comfort.'

'I try,' he said, starting to drive down the broad street again. 'I've always liked a luxury car.'

'This surely is one,' she said, taking in the upholstery and expensive metal work inside.

His eyes were fixed on the traffic ahead. 'It will cool off in a few minutes.'

She said, 'I don't mind the heat.'

'I gathered that,' he said dryly. 'Or you wouldn't have been out walking in the sun just now.'

She looked at his profile. 'Why aren't you at the races?'

'I decided to take the day off.'

'Can trainers do that?'

'Occasionally.'

'And you are a trainer, aren't you?' she said, anxious to trap him in a lie.

He gave her a good-humored glance. 'As a matter of fact I lied to you. I'm not a trainer.'

He'd spoiled her game. She said, 'Why did you lie to me?'

'I hated to have to admit that I was a gambler.'

'I see.'

'Some people don't consider us too respectable,' he went on. 'Actually I'm beyond reproach.'

'I'm sure you are,' she said somewhat acidly. 'Now I won't know what to believe about you. You lie so well.'

He winced. 'And I did it only to keep your good opinion of me.'

'It hasn't turned out well.'

'So it seems.'

She said, 'I have another little matter to discuss with you. I consider it somewhat more important. In fact, it's another case in which it appears you deliberately lied to me.'

Cal Wayne said, 'There's a parking spot just ahead on the left. Suppose we stop by there.'

'Anywhere will do!' she told him angrily.

He gave the car a spurt of gas and then headed off the road to the parking area which was largely deserted at this time of day.

'I'm allowing the motor to idle so I can keep the air-conditioning on,' he explained. Now gazing across at her he added, 'You seem in a taut mood.'

'I suppose I am in one.'

'What about?'

'Another lie.'

'Go on,' he said.

'This has to do with David Barry,' she told him.

'That's why I came in a hurry to find you. I've heard from Nick. He didn't like you nosing around his place.'

'I gathered that.'

163

'It was stupid to do it. You didn't learn anything more than you were told by me. And you exposed yourself to plenty of danger.'

'You think so?' she said airily.

'I know you did.'

'Then why did you offer me that story in the first place?'

He looked uneasy. 'I was right. David Barry is dead.'

'Your David Barry is. Not mine!'

'How can you say that?' He seemed honestly shocked.

'It's true!'

'How did you come to that conclusion?'

'I have some proof,' she told him.

He stared at her. 'You don't care how much trouble you land yourself into!'

'Why did you tell me *my* David Barry was dead?'

He studied her in silence for a moment. Then he told her, 'All right. I'll admit I fed you that bit about Barry being dead to get rid of you. I hoped you'd be discouraged and get out of Saratoga.'

'But I didn't!'

'No,' he said bitterly. 'You sure didn't. Rushing off to see Nick Lucas was one of the dumbest things you ever tried.'

'Why?'

'Nick doesn't like nosey young women,' the man sitting beside her said. 'And then you went on to see that crazy cousin!'

164

'Bertha?'

'Right! Bertha! There's a girl who is bad news.'

'What's wrong with her?' Andrea asked. 'She behaved so oddly!'

Cal Wayne looked grim. 'She's on dope! Has been for some time. She was waiting for a delivery when you came along!'

All the strange behavior of the unfortunate woman came rushing back into her mind. And she realized that it had been fairly obvious, only she hadn't gotten on to it because she hadn't been looking for it.

She said, 'So that's why she was acting so oddly.'

'That's why,' the young man said in a grim voice. 'And you had to rush there and get mixed up in it.'

'How do you know I was there and, anyway, I'm not mixed up in it,' she protested.

'You may think not,' Cal Wayne told her. 'But that man with the stuff from Joe was standing across the street watching you. He waited until he was sure you had left and then he saw Bertha and made her tell him what you were up to. These dope people can't afford to take any risks.'

She began to see what he meant. She said, 'I wouldn't have gone either place if you hadn't told me David Barry was dead.'

'I was sure that news alone would be enough to get you on your way. That you'd say goodbye to Saratoga and the Ansonia right away.'

Andrea shook her head. 'I had to find more out about David Barry, even if he were dead.'

'You're sure it wasn't the same Barry?'

'You know it wasn't!' she protested. 'You've admitted it.'

He shrugged. 'Still, I wondered if by some small chance it would turn out he was the same person. Just what does this David Barry mean to you?' the man in the dark glasses asked.

'I don't have to answer that,' she said. 'But I will. At least to a point. He's a good friend of mine. It may even be that I love him.'

Wayne gave a low whistle. 'You didn't make that plain enough earlier. If that's the case, you want my advice?'

'What?'

'Leave Saratoga. If this Barry wants to find you, he will. Give him time. You're placing yourself in needless danger staying on here.'

She gave him a sharp look. 'How do you know that?'

'The Ansonia Hotel is not a healthy place for young women during the racing season.'

Andrea was shocked at his being so blunt. She decided on some bluntness of her own. She said, 'What do you know about the attack on me last night?'

He showed surprise. And if he were putting on an act she decided it was a good one. He said, 'I didn't know anything about it until just now.'

'You expect me to believe that?'

'You may as well,' he said. 'It's true.'

'You bluff so well,' she said cautiously, not convinced of his sincerity yet.

'Tell me about it,' he said.

'Need I?'

'Don't be so nasty-smart,' he reprimanded her. 'I want to hear about last night.'

She told him. 'I could have been the third silk-stocking murder victim,' she said as she finished her account.

Cal Wayne studied her grimly. 'And you think I may be the killer?'

'I don't know what to think about you.'

'That's flattering.'

'Is there any reason why I shouldn't be suspicious of you?'

'I'm wondering why you should.'

'You lie to me,' she said. 'And I know nothing about what you're doing here.'

He said, 'You don't know much more about Monty Freeman. Yet you seem to trust him in everything.'

'Why shouldn't I?'

'I'll give you one reason,' the young man in the car seat beside her said bitterly. 'He was in the hotel last night and I wasn't. Further, by his own admission he left the lounge just before you were attacked and returned afterward. Who can say that he didn't go up on the fire escape and try to throttle you?'

It was a possibility which had never occurred to her before. Monty had been so positive about his efforts to help her. He'd told about his leaving the lounge and starting upstairs then changing his mind at the second level. And he'd taken the stairs rather than the elevator! How easy it would have been for him to have slipped out onto the fire escape by a hall window and make his way up to her room on the outside of the building! But she didn't want to believe it!'

'No!' she protested.

'Why not?' Cal Wayne asked with a bitter smile. 'Why must I always be suspected while you refuse to think anything wrong about him? Is it because he has poisoned your mind about me?'

'Why would he want to kill me?'

'Why would I?'

She was caught off balance. She said, 'I don't know. The killer must be mad! Or perhaps it is the ghost of the original killer after all!'

The sturdy young man in the dark glasses laughed harshly. 'It seems you'd rather believe in a ghost than accept that Monty Freeman could be a homicidal maniac.'

'He's a very gentle young man!'

'So are many killers until they're found out!'

'I just don't think he could do it.'

'But I might? Is that it?'

'I'm not blaming you either,' she protested.

'But I don't feel I know you as well. And after all the lies you offered me about yourself and about David Barry being dead!'

'I admitted my lies.'

'Not until I caught you in them!' she reminded him. She felt terribly confused and no longer certain of anything.

'All right,' he said somewhat wearily. 'Think your worst about me if you like. But do me a favor.'

'What?'

'Try and learn something more about Monty Freeman.'

'How?'

He smiled grimly. 'You seem to have quite a knack for finding out things. You didn't take long to begin questioning Nick Lucas and that Bertha.'

'I knew about them.'

'Well, try working on Monty,' the self-confessed gambler told her. 'As a start I'll give you a few clues.'

'What sort of clues?'

His eyes met hers. 'You have some new guests at the hotel.'

'We have a lot of guests.'

'Not so many that you won't notice these new ones. There is a dark gangster type, a battered ex-pug and a pretty girl who dresses too loudly.'

Her eyes widened. 'You mean Al Moroni and his friends.'

Cal nodded. 'You catch on fast.'

'What about them?'

'They've come to the hotel for a special reason,' Cal Wayne said. 'Don't ever mention that I told you this. But it's true.'

'What sort of reason?'

'It could have something to do with that piano player.'

'Monty?' she gasped.

'He's the only piano player at the hotel.'

'I don't believe it,' she protested.

Cal looked grim again. 'Have you ever seen them talking to him?'

She hesitated. 'What do you mean?'

'Just what I said,' he told her evenly. 'Have you ever seen that trio of crooks talking to Monty?'

She couldn't reply. She remembered all too well how they had halted by Monty in the dining room and insisted that they knew him. That they'd met before. And he'd attempted to deny it!

CHAPTER EIGHT

Cal Wayne said, 'You haven't answered me.'

She emerged from her suspicious thoughts to say, 'Al Moroni did speak to him.'

'I thought so,' he said triumphantly.

'I'm sure it didn't mean anything.'

'What did Moroni say to him?'

'He wondered if they hadn't met somewhere. Monty seemed to feel it was because Moroni had seen him working in some New York night spot.'

'Maybe working for Moroni,' Cal Wayne suggested.

'No. I don't believe that!' she protested.

'They could be in collusion,' he said. 'I suggest you keep your eyes open.'

'What about you?' she asked defiantly. 'What am I to think about you?'

'That I'm trying to be your friend.'

'You don't behave much like it,' she said. 'You're always upsetting me.'

'By suggesting what may be entirely possible,' he replied to her. 'I'm going to drive on to the racetrack restaurant. We still have time for a cold drink before you need to go back to the hotel.'

'I don't know,' she said.

He laughed as he headed the car out of the parking area. 'Surely you're not afraid to be seen with me?'

'It's not that.'

'Then there's no reason why we shouldn't be seen in public together,' he said as he drove in the direction of the big track.

When they reached the track he ignored the races to take her directly into the lounge. After they had found a table and were served he gave her a knowing glance.

'Have you ever considered how completely dependent on the races Saratoga is now?' he asked.

'That's pretty evident when you look around you today,' she agreed.

He nodded. 'You saw the thousands of people in the stands, the parking areas crowded with cars, and this place is jammed. It all adds up. Saratoga is the track! When the trotting ends in October it becomes a kind of ghost town.'

'There's something of a lost splendor about it even in season,' Andrea said. 'The Ansonia is an example. I'm sure it was once very up-to-date and filled with fashionable people. There's nothing here to take its place.'

'Just the one luxury hotel,' Cal Wayne said. 'And that's for a special few. This Holiday Inn built overlooking the tracks was an inspiration. And it suits the modern trend. Have you any idea what kind of a busy day most of the racing people have here?'

'No.'

172

'It begins about seven in the morning and ends maybe by midnight,' Cal Wayne said. 'There are try-outs to watch in the morning, sales to attend, the races in the afternoon during August. The rules call for twenty-one days of major racing every year. There can be no deviation from that.'

She smiled. 'You're very knowledgeable and enthusiastic for someone who merely gambles on the horses.'

'I was a trainer once,' he said. 'I have a real feeling for the game. But the days of trainers representing a half-dozen stables are dying out. I lost my job and turned to betting.'

'You don't seem the type,' she told him.

'Is there any type?' he asked. 'I follow the tracks in season. So far I've been lucky.'

'What about Slim Gordon?'

'The jockey?'

'Yes. You've been at the hotel a lot together.'

'I know,' Cal said. 'I have to go easy on that. He is a respected jockey and it sort of looks bad having him seen with me too often. Any suspicion that we were working together could do him a lot of harm. I won't be seeing him for a while for that reason.'

'But you are good friends?'

'Sure. Dates back to when I was a trainer. But I have to be careful during the time he's racing. We see each other between seasons.'

The explanation sounded reasonable and

yet she still wasn't certain that he was being completely truthful with her. She liked him just as she liked Monty. But she felt she did not know him as well as she did the pianist.

She said, 'I must soon start back. If we get caught in the traffic from the track I'll be late.'

'We'll leave right away,' Cal Wayne said. And he signalled for his check.

On the drive back, he asked her, 'Have the hotel people told the police about the attack on you last night?'

'No,' she said.

'They should have,' Cal said with a frown on his tanned face. 'They're taking a chance otherwise.'

'Mr. Clayton seemed to feel it would be better to keep it to ourselves for the moment.'

'It sounds like Clayton is taking a whole lot better care of his hotel than he is of you,' the young man at the wheel said bitterly.

'He may be right, you know,' she said seriously. 'I had so little to give in evidence.'

'I still say he's wrong,' Cal complained.

They reached the hotel and he let her out. As she walked up to the front entrance she saw Monty standing on the verandah. And she knew he must have seen her leave Cal's sporty white sedan. She mounted the steps to the verandah with her cheeks burning.

Monty came to greet her. With an ironic expression he said, 'Been out seeing the sights?'

'I just met Cal and talked a little.'

'I gathered that,' he said, glancing in the direction in which the car had gone. Then he looked at her again. 'I thought you were of the opinion Cal Wayne might be the one who'd made that attack on you.'

She shook her head. 'I don't think so anymore.'

'Oh, he's explained everything satisfactorily?' the young pianist said with sarcasm.

She blushed more furiously. 'Don't be difficult,' she asked him.

'I can't help it,' he said. 'After all our discussion about Wayne I find you with him.'

'I had to hear his explanations,' she told him.

'I'll bet they were something,' Monty said sarcastically. 'I'm satisfied at what he told me,' she said. 'There are times when you haven't been as clear in what you've told me.'

'Now I'm the one at fault!'

'I didn't say that!'

'You hinted it clearly enough,' Monty said, still in a tone of anger.

She was unable to restrain asking him, 'What about you and Al Moroni?'

Monty seemed stunned. 'What about it?'

'I think you know him better than you care to admit,' she answered.

'You can think what you like,' the young man said. 'I told you the truth about him. He's

175

seen me somewhere. That's all!'

'I hope that's all, Monty,' she said quietly. 'I have to go change for work.' And she passed him and went on inside.

She was surprised to find the tall Olaf operating the elevator. The big man nodded to her and studied her from behind his glasses with his large sad eyes.

'You have a good day, Miss?' he asked.

'I guess so,' she said. 'What about you? I understood you had been relieved of your other duties to concentrate as night watchman.'

'Yes, Miss. But when someone doesn't show up they think of me,' he said in his doleful sing-song. 'Mike did not show up today. So I have had to work the elevator part time. And Grant has taken turns with it.'

She said, 'Grant is a strange person. Very quiet and yet he seems an intelligent old man.'

'Grant has been around hotels a long time,' Olaf observed. 'He is lonely and makes no friends with anyone else who works here. He hardly speaks two words to me.'

'I know what he can be like,' she agreed. Olaf let her off at the fourth floor and she rushed to her room and put on a gown for the dining room.

When she went downstairs Edna was already on duty. The white-haired woman studied her for a few seconds and said, 'I think you're looking better.'

176

'I feel better,' she agreed.

'Mr. Clayton has been wanting to see you,' Edna told her.

'Oh? Anything about last night?'

'It may be,' the small woman in the white smock said. 'He was very mysterious as usual. You know what he's like.'

She stood there with the menus in hand, uncertain what she should do. She said, 'Do you think I should go to his office now?'

'No,' Edna said. 'He'll be coming in for his own dinner and he'll offer you any news he has, then.'

'Yes. That would be the best time,' Andrea agreed.

For the next twenty minutes she was busy greeting guests and showing them to their tables. The older guests of the hotel all knew her now and most of them enjoyed exchanging a few words with her as they were seated. The newcomers had to be shown to tables kept for transients.

Mr. Clayton arrived after the first rush. He nodded to her. The stout man seemed tense. He said, 'After dinner I have something I'd like you to do for me. I'll explain to you later. Drop by my office when you finish in here.'

'I'll be glad to,' she agreed, mystified at what he might want.

He went on to the staff table as she turned to find Al Moroni waiting for his table. He was alone and the sleek, swarthy man had an impatient air.

'I guess you remember me,' the dark-haired man said arrogantly.

'I do, Mr. Moroni,' she said politely. 'Sorry I kept you waiting. Where are the others?'

'They'll be along soon,' he said.

'I'll show you to your table,' Andrea told him. And she led him to his table and pulled out a chair for him.

As he sat down he glanced up at her. 'I saw you at the Holiday Inn lounge this afternoon.'

'Oh?'

'Yeah,' he said, staring up at her significantly. 'I got quite a kick out of that. You were with Wayne. Cal Wayne.'

'Yes. Do you know him?'

The swarthy Moroni smiled nastily. 'Let's say I've heard about him. Saratoga is a small town. News gets around quick. I guess he stays here, doesn't he?'

'He has a room at the Ansonia,' she agreed.

'Must keep an eye open for him,' Moroni said. 'If I don't connect with him maybe you'll take him a message from me. By the look of you two today you have to be good friends.'

She was angered at his impertinence but covered her feelings and said, 'I must get back to the door. Some people are waiting.'

'Sure,' Moroni said with a knowing wink. 'We can talk later. I'd like that.'

Andrea ignored his remark and went to the entrance to show a young couple to a nearby

178

table. When she returned to the hallway Monty Freeman began playing the piano again. He had been studiously avoiding her since their argument on the verandah. It seemed that everyone in the hotel knew she'd been out with Cal Wayne.

She was still standing in the entrance way to the dining room awaiting guests when Jake Gotell and the girl she knew only as Rose arrived. She quickly showed them to Moroni's table and left all three talking in low, confidential tones. The balance of the dinner hour proved uneventful. She went back to the staff table as early as she could and had a light dinner. By that time Monty had finished playing.

When her dinner was over she checked the evening's receipts with Edna and then left for the manager's office as Ernest Clayton had requested. She found him seated at his desk. When he saw her he at once rose and offered her a chair.

'Good of you to come by so soon, Miss Gibbs,' the stout man said.

'We just finished in the dining room.'

He beamed across the desk at her. 'I must congratulate you on the way you have handled things there. You've got the place running very smoothly.'

'Edna has been a great help,' she said. 'In fact she taught me much of what I'm doing.'

'Wonderful woman, Edna,' the manager

agreed. 'But she did need help. And you have proven ideal.'

'Thank you,' she said politely, wondering what the pompous little man had in mind. 'You wanted to see me.'

He cleared his throat. 'Yes. That is so. I'm deeply grateful that you made no fuss about last night's unfortunate happening. I have lectured Olaf on his security duties and I'm sure you need have no fears in the future.'

'That is good news,' she said, though privately she debated how much it meant.

'There is another thing,' Ernest Clayton said with a frown.

She saw how tense he was and wondered. 'Yes?' she said.

'We have a guest here I do not believe you've met,' the manager told her.

'Really?'

'Yes. She never goes to the dining room for meals. In fact she spends a great deal of her stay here in her own suite of rooms on the second floor. Her name is Mrs. Catherine Flanders.'

'I never have heard of her.'

'I didn't think so,' the manager said carefully. His eyes met Andrea's. 'But as it happens she has heard of you.'

'Oh?' She was surprised.

The manager looked embarrassed. 'I'm afraid it is my fault. I visit Mrs. Flanders each day. She spends a lot of money with the hotel.

180

Her suite is the most expensive in the house. And so I give her personal attention. She takes a great interest in what goes on here and I tell her everything I feel will be of interest. Unhappily, I mentioned the attack on you last night, knowing it would go no further with her, and frankly I needed to talk to someone about it. At once she requested that I send you up to see her. I have no idea why.'

'That is strange.'

'Very. But she is an unusual person. A beauty in her day. She married a rather old man. They began staying here in the good days of the hotel about thirty-five years ago. She has not missed a summer yet though her husband has been long dead.'

'That's an amazing story,' she said.

Ernest Clayton rubbed his head nervously and said, 'The rich are eccentric. I have learned that in my years in the hotel business. Mrs. Flanders is a key example. She keeps her suite in near darkness. The shades are always drawn and she uses very few lights even at night. She appears to enjoy living in a kind of twilight zone. You will find the suite in near darkness.'

'It sounds eerie.'

'It is an eerie atmosphere,' the manager agreed. 'She has one old female servant who has been with her for years and an elderly chauffeur who stays in the chauffeur's quarters over the stables. Anyway, she has asked to

181

meet you. Would you mind?'

'Should I go up there now?'

The manager drummed the stubby fingers of his right hand on the desktop. 'Yes, I suppose so,' he sighed. 'If she goes into details in questioning you about the attack on you last night please try to play it down to her. I would appreciate that.'

'Very well,' she said. 'You have an idea she may fear an attack on herself next?'

'I'm not sure,' the manager admitted. 'I'd consider the possibility of it very slight. In any case I'd appreciate it if you'd go up and see what she wants and forgive me for babbling to strangers about your misadventure.'

'I'd best go now,' she said, still unsure what it was all about.

Olaf took her up to the second floor in the elevator. He looked tired and haggard and she felt he was being worked too hard for his age. She went down the hall until she came to the entrance door of the suite. There she rang a bell and waited what seemed an endless time for someone to answer.

At last there were footsteps on the other side of the door and it was opened by a bent woman with iron-gray hair in a maid's cap and uniform.

'Yes?' the maid inquired.

'Mrs. Flanders is expecting me,' she said. 'I'm Andrea Gibbs.'

'Oh, yes!' the elderly maid said, stepping

182

aside. 'Do come on in.'

She entered the suite and found it exactly as the hotel manager had described it. There was little light. The blinds and drapes had been drawn and only a few scattered lamps had been left turned on.

The maid said, 'Mrs. Flanders is in the other room. Just follow me.'

She did and a moment later found herself in what seemed a study. There, seated in a chair by a table draped in black, was a tall, slender woman with closely cropped gray hair and a thin, melancholy face. Yet it was a face of distinction which hinted of a former beauty. Now dark shadows under the eyes and hollows in her cheeks had faded the looks of the older woman.

Seeing Andrea, the woman, who was dressed all in black, rose from her chair and offered her hand to Andrea, saying, 'Of course you must be Miss Gibbs.'

'Yes,' she said in a small voice, overwhelmed by the oddity of her surroundings.

The woman gestured to a chair across the small table from her. 'Do sit down,' she said.

Andrea did so. She offered hesitantly, 'This is an unusual apartment.'

'You mean the darkness, I presume,' Mrs. Flanders said. 'I keep it this way because too much light bothers me. I prefer the shadows. Do you mind the room?'

'No,' she said, though a tiny chill had

183

coursed through her.

The only lights in the room were two candle-like fixtures on the wall and they gave off only a dull glow which did little to dispel the shadows of the place. She could barely make out the face and figure of the woman seated across from her at the small, black-draped table.

Mrs. Catherine Flanders offered her a melancholy smile and said, 'I suppose you wonder why I have asked you here.'

'Mr. Clayton told me you would like to see me,' she said, nervously.

'That is so,' the older woman said. 'Dear Mr. Clayton is a great comfort to me. And he told me about your experience last night. I prefer to think of it as a visitation.'

'A visitation?' she repeated, staring at the woman in the shadows.

'Yes. A visit from a ghost. You see I'm a great believer in spiritualism,' Mrs. Flanders explained. And then in a dramatic gesture she yanked the black cloth covering the table away to show a glowing crystal ball on the table between them. The ball was illuminated by some fixture installed underneath it and its light served to highlight the worn, melancholy features of Mrs. Flanders.

'You have a crystal ball,' she ventured.

'Yes,' the older woman said. 'And occasionally I seek and find answers in it. I regret that for some days now it has been

184

cloudy and I have been able to discern nothing.'

'Is that usual?'

'Only when the spirits are vexed,' Mrs. Flanders said. 'And I suspect they are angry with me now.' She spoke these words in a hushed voice.

'I'm afraid I know little about such things,' she said, cold running down her spine again. There was something about this tall woman in black and her sad manner which had a ghostly taint.

Mrs. Flanders smiled sadly. 'Of course you do not understand. I will try and explain. Last night you were attacked by an unseen intruder as I understand it?'

'Yes.'

'And an attempt was made to strangle you with a silk stocking just as has happened here on three occasions before,' she said in a taut voice.

'Yes. I think so.'

The woman's eyes were shining oddly. 'That is what Mr. Clayton told me. I'm sure he afterward regretted being so brash but I was grateful to him. I wanted to meet you. Because you see there is a link between us.'

'A link?'

'Yes,' the woman said in her sad voice. 'I have been a guest at this hotel every season for thirty-five years. That means I was here when the first silk-stocking murder was committed.

When James Dennis was imprisoned for the crime, that poor deaf and dumb young man. He was torn from his wife and two children for a crime he could not have committed.'

Andrea was shocked. 'Could not have committed?'

'No,' Mrs. Flanders said. 'I knew James Dennis when I was growing up. We were both of middle class families. I married well and rose above my station in life. Because of his affliction James had to take a job unworthy of him. When I came to this hotel with my late husband, Major Flanders, I learned that James was employed here as a kind of handyman. I found out that he and his wife and kiddies lived in a house on the hotel grounds. In due time I met him one evening when I was out for a stroll.'

'And he recognized you?'

'Yes,' the woman in black said. 'It had not been that many years since we were in our teens together in our home town. I was a young woman and beautiful then, so I've been told. I was also very lonely. And I was married to a much older man, a stern man who spent much of his time away from me taking care of his business activities. You may be able to guess what happened.'

'There was a summer romance between you and James Dennis?'

The older woman nodded, her melancholy face showing distress. 'Heaven forgive me, yes!

I was so sorry for Dennis and I believed myself in love with him. I forgot about his wife and two youngsters. We arranged for him to come secretly to my suite, this same suite we are in now. It was easy for him to get away from his wife with the excuse of having chores to do at the hotel. This thing between us went on most of the summer. One week when my husband came here to stay I did not see James. But the rest of the time we contrived to be together several nights a week.'

'What about the woman who was murdered?'

'She was a hussy,' Catherine Flanders said angrily. 'She had her eye on James too. He told me how she'd tried to get him to make love to her. But poor James would have nothing to do with her. He loved me. She played a dangerous game with others in the hotel and then she was murdered. And because James could not prove where he was at the time and because of other incriminating evidence which alone meant little, he was arrested and tried for the murder. A murder he did not do because he was with me when it happened.'

There was a hush in the shadowed room. Andrea found it almost impossible to make a comment. At last in a hushed voice, she said, 'You knew this young man did not kill that other woman and yet you kept silent and let him take the blame for it.'

'It was what he wanted me to do,' Catherine Flanders exclaimed unhappily. 'He let me know that. I could not admit to the truth. I would have been completely ruined. My husband would never have forgiven me. I would have lost everything!'

She stared at the dark-clad figure in the shadows with her ruined face spotlighted by the crystal ball. She said, 'But you let him lose everything. And you say you loved him!'

'I did love him,' the woman said in a frantic tone. 'I did! You must believe that! But I needed to think it over. Get the courage to act.'

'And you never did?'

'I planned it. James went to jail. I gave money to his wife and children. Saw they were given a good start in another city. My husband applauded me for my kindness. I was so ashamed. I knew I soon had to admit to the truth.'

'But you still hesitated?'

The woman in black sighed. 'Fate stepped in. My husband became ill. His doctors told me the disease was terminal and that he would die within a year. I knew then what I would do. I would wait until his death and I had inherited the estate. Then I would go to my lawyer and confess everything and we would see that James Dennis received a new trial.'

'And?'

'My husband lingered on,' Mrs. Flanders

said. 'He was two years dying rather than one. And before his death finally came I received word that James Dennis had contracted pneumonia in prison and died within a week. It was a month later my husband died. After that I had a nervous collapse and was in a hospital for months. When I came out I determined to find James's wife and children and make them wealthy. But in the interim she had changed her name and vanished. I was not able to locate them. And so down through the years I have lived with my guilt and tried to reach James in the spirit world and ask his forgiveness.'

'Why have you told me all this?' Andrea asked.

'Because you are involved.'

'How?'

'I have kept coming to the Ansonia for all these years because it is here I think I may one time make a contact with James on the other side. The finest spiritualists have tried to help me reach him without avail. But I still return here and hope.'

'That is why you keep the place so dark and see no one?'

'While I am here I give all my time and energy to attempting to talk to James in that other world. I must somehow explain to him.'

Andrea began to realize the woman was mad though not dangerous. She said, 'You have had no success at all?'

'Once or twice I have been close but there is a barrier between us,' the woman said sadly. 'In his anger the spirit of my beloved James has gone mad. So that two years ago he returned in ghostly form and killed a guest here, a lovely looking girl, and last year one of the most attractive of the maids was found strangled in the same manner out by the shuffleboard. Last night it was to have been your turn. Only a miracle saved you from dying at the hands of my beloved James!'

'You're saying it was his mad ghost that returned to kill me?'

'Yes. As he killed those other two.'

She stared at the eerie figure of Mrs. Flanders crouched over the glowing crystal ball and felt both sadness and revulsion for her. It was a love of money which had kept Catherine Flanders from telling the truth and saving the man she claimed to have loved. Greed for wealth and position had ruined her and doomed her to this madness of endless days and nights in shadow.

She said, 'I'm afraid I can't accept that theory.'

'But you must!' the other woman exclaimed.

'You are sure that James Dennis was innocent?'

'Yes.'

Andrea said slowly, 'Then who did kill that girl all those years ago?'

'I don't know,' Mrs. Flanders said uneasily.

'It had to be someone else.'

'And you helped that someone else escape the penalty for that crime,' she told the elderly woman sternly.

'What?' The woman gasped as if this had never struck her before.

Andrea said, 'You allowed a killer to go free. And for all we know he may still be alive and committing these new murders. It doesn't have to be the angry spirit of James Dennis that is to blame.'

Catherine Flanders's melancholy face had taken on a look of distress. 'Don't say such things!' she begged her.

'I must,' she said. 'You are guilty in more than one way. What about this criminal who escaped? Do you have any idea who it might have been?'

'No,' she said in a hushed voice. 'No idea at all. That girl had been carrying on with a lot of men. Mr. Clayton knows about it. He was here as assistant manager in those days. And Grant was here. He was the social director then. He was young and handsome, not like he is now. And she knew him. James was sure those two were more that friendly. Ask Grant about her.'

These revelations had stunned Andrea. But she managed to keep a casual front and say, 'I will ask Grant. He may remember who was here then and who might be the criminal.'

'In the meantime you must try and protect yourself against the ghost,' the woman in black told her.

She rose from the chair. 'I will remember,' she promised.

Catherine Flanders also got to her feet and came over to her. 'Perhaps if we both called on the crystal ball it would clear and we might get our answer from James,' she suggested.

'I told you, Mrs. Flanders. I do not believe in spiritualism,' she said.

The older woman looked shocked. 'You are so wrong, my child.'

'I don't blame you for clinging to it if it helps you,' she told her. 'I feel no need of it.'

'Wait!' the woman in black warned her. 'One day you will!'

'We'll see,' Andrea said, making her way through the near darkness to the living room. She wanted most to get away from the oppressive darkness and the grim evil of Catherine Flanders. She found the doorknob and turned it to open the door and let herself out into the corridor.

CHAPTER NINE

She moved slowly along the shadowed corridor of the old hotel. Clayton and Grant! They were the two who had been with the hotel at the time of the murder in the thirties. It was amazing that they were still in the employ of the same firm. And it could mean something that they had remained so long with this particular hotel chain.

Her talk with Catherine Flanders had put an entirely new light on that long-ago crime. Now it seemed much closer and much more real to her. She buzzed for the elevator and then waited until it came up creaking and groaning to get her.

Olaf opened the door for her. 'Evening, Miss Gibbs,' he said.

She stepped into the elevator. 'Didn't Mike get back yet?'

'No, Miss. When he takes it into his head to go on a drinking spell he is usually gone a day or two.'

'Is that what has happened?' she asked.

'I'm afraid so,' the big elderly man said and gave his full attention to the elevator.

They reached the ground floor and she got out after thanking him. Then she went on to the office of the manager. When she got there the little man looked up from his desk at her like a rosy, innocent cherub.

'How did you make out with her?'

'All right up to a point,' she said.

The stout man looked less happy. 'She isn't easy. I warned you of that.'

'The woman is mad.'

Ernest Clayton gasped and held up a silencing hand. 'We must not have that sort of talk about our guests.'

'It's unfortunate but it's true,' she insisted.

The stout man said, 'Mrs. Flanders does no one any harm and the hotel wants to protect her.'

'Hasn't she been protected too long?' Andrea asked. 'What do you mean?'

'I think you know,' she said.

'If you're referring to the murder,' the manager said, 'I can tell you Catherine is innocent.'

'I realize that but if neither she nor James Dennis could have been guilty of that crime, the guilty party was left free to live on unharmed all these years. It doesn't seem fair!'

'What can I do about it?'

'I can't tell you right at the moment,' she said. 'But there must be some way now to find out who the guilty one is. And I understand you and Grant were both here in the hotel when the killing was done.'

'I remember it well enough,' Ernest Clayton said, suddenly looking older. 'I tried to unravel the plot but got nowhere. It looks to remain a mystery.'

She said, 'You must have had some thoughts about who did the crime.'

The stout man stared dismally at his desk top for a long moment. Then, as if having made up his mind, he raised his head. 'I guess I'd be a liar if I said I didn't suspect anyone. Because maybe I do.'

'And you've also kept silent all these years?' she asked in surprise.

Ernest Clayton nodded his bald head. 'You have friends and don't want to involve them.'

She gazed at the little bald man with unflinching eyes. And she asked, 'Whom do you suspect?'

He hesitated and then rather miserably, he told her, 'Grant. He's changed so over the years. Become a completely opposite kind of person from what he was. And he did see a lot of that girl who was murdered. I've always suspected Grant.'

'Grant!' she repeated in a tense voice. And she pictured the wreck of an elderly man with his sallow face and shifty eyes who worked as night clerk. It was impossible for her to identify him with the bright, young social director he was said to have been thirty-five years earlier.

The stout Ernest Clayton leaned across his desk and spoke in a low voice, 'Grant and the murdered girl were close. Then I believe they had a quarrel. It was after that she became the

195

'first victim of the silk-stocking murderer.'

'And after that Grant changed?'

'Slowly,' the manager said. 'I didn't notice it at first. But over the years the change became marked. He drank heavily for a period and had a stomach operation. After that he was never the same. He remained as emaciated and hostile as he is today. The company found a position for him where he wouldn't be in too much contact with the public.'

'You think the change may have been caused by his conscience as a killer who got off without paying for his crime?' she said.

'Yes.'

'What about the recent murders?'

'I don't know,' the manager admitted. 'I can't see Grant as a murderer today. He isn't agile enough. In any case I don't know how we'd go about proving anything.'

Andrea frowned. 'That is the difficult thing. You could start with Mrs. Flanders's confession and her evidence that James Dennis couldn't have committed the first murder. That would at least clear his name and be a beginning.'

The paunchy Ernest Clayton shook his bald head. 'There's not a hope there,' he said.

She stared at him in surprise. 'What do you mean?'

The manager said earnestly, 'Ever since Catherine Flanders had her break-down following her husband's death her affairs have been looked after by a picked group of executors.'

'Meaning what?'

'In the eyes of any court she could not be accepted as completely sane,' he said very slowly. 'Her testimony would be worthless.'

Andrea was shocked. 'You're certain of this?'

'The hotel is paid by her attorneys,' Ernest Clayton said. 'Her attorneys make her bookings here for her. And when it is time for her to return to her home they make sure that all the details are attended to.'

'In other words she is regarded as mad but not mentally ill enough to be in an institution?'

'If she were less wealthy it might be required to place her in some sort of sanitarium. But she has the money to pay for being cared for on the outside.'

Her eyes were wide with the enormity of this revelation. She said, 'If that is the case then that story she tells about James Dennis being her lover and with her at the time the murder was committed, may be all a figment of her sick imagination.'

The manager nodded. 'That is it exactly.'

'She told the story so convincingly!'

'And it may be true. But no one will listen to her evidence,' the manager said. 'That is why nothing has been done about it all these years. I'm sorry I had to expose you to her. But at least you've seen what a dreadful mental state

197

she is in.'

'I can't believe her suite is kept in darkness day and night,' she said. 'It's eerie just going in there briefly.'

'I agree,' Ernest Clayton said. 'It is even more difficult for me. I also remember her as a lovely, vivacious young woman, not the melancholy wraith she has become.'

'There must be something in her story,' Andrea insisted. 'Otherwise she would not have changed so.'

'I'm inclined to agree. But how to prove it?'

She sighed. 'It's true the chances are small.'

'That first murder is lost in the past,' the manager said. 'Most of the chief figures in it are dead, or aging and a little mad. I don't think it's important that we learn the whole truth about it.'

She stared at him. 'You surprise me. I think finding out the truth about a murder is always important.'

The stout man looked somewhat flustered. 'I didn't intend to underestimate the importance of justice being done. What I meant is that it is much more urgent now that we learn the truth about what is behind these two more recent murders and the attack on you.'

'Mrs. Flanders lays all three to the ghost of James Dennis,' she said disgustedly.

'Mrs. Flanders is mad. There must be some other explanation.'

'I think Monty Freeman came up with the best theory. He believes some modern psychotic has taken on the identity of the silk-stocking murderer after hearing the legend. Probably we can blame such throwbacks in crime to the current nostalgia craze. It even touches off the insane.'

'Freeman could be right,' the manager agreed. 'It makes an easy explanation whether it is the right one or not.'

'And you have no ideas?' she asked him.

The manager lowered his voice again. 'Unless it is Grant. It may be he was guilty of the first murder and now he is repeating his madness.'

'He should be watched carefully,' she said.

The stout Ernest Clayton spread his hands. 'There is very little I can do. The police would never listen to the vague theory I have to offer concerning his guilt. But I have asked Olaf to keep an eye on him without telling him why.'

'Perhaps you should let Olaf know the truth,' she worried.

'I doubt if that would do any good,' the manager said. 'Olaf has a limited intelligence. He would be confused. As things stand now he'll keep an eye on Grant without being bothered about his motives for doing so.'

'I suppose you know your staff best,' she admitted.

'That is so,' Ernest Clayton agreed. 'You've met Mrs. Flanders and heard her story.'

'What will I do if she invites me to her suite again?'

'You'll have to make the decision for yourself,' the manager said. 'It might be well to try and keep her placated. At the same time you can't become a martyr to a mad-woman.'

She smiled ruefully. 'The Ansonia houses more strange secrets than I guessed.'

'This old hotel has seen many strange things,' the manager said soberly. 'And perhaps there are more to come.'

'I hope not. At least not while I'm here,' she said. And she got up.

The manager rose. 'You understand that all this is confidential between us. I do not want gossip about Mrs. Flanders to go further. She is our guest and under our protection.'

'I will keep that in mind,' she said quietly.

The stout little man accompanied her to the door of his office. 'You are comfortable in your new room?'

'Yes.'

'I don't think you'll be in the same danger there,' he told her.

'I hope not.'

'Olaf is also going to give your safety his special attention,' the manager said. 'I don't think we'll have any recurrence of that unpleasantness.'

'I'm counting on that,' she said.

The manager gazed at her with appraising eyes. 'I find you a unique person, Miss Gibbs. I consider the hotel was fortunate in securing your services.'

She left him on this upbeat note. In the lobby she saw that most of the older guests had already gone up to bed. In one area Al Moroni, Jake and Rose were standing together talking and there was a scattering of younger people about. She let her eyes wander to the desk and saw that Grant was on duty.

The shabby sallow-faced old man was giving some information to a guest and did not see her. She stared at his thin face and wondered about whether he was a murderer or not. She had become so caught up in the silk-stocking murders that she'd almost forgotten her real reason for coming to Saratoga. She had come here to find David Barry and thus far she'd drawn a blank.

It was possible the young newspaperman was no longer in the city. If so, she'd made her journey for nothing. But she still had hopes of his turning up. And she heard Monty playing in the lounge and once again wondered whether the young pianist might be her secret computer-love. There were moments when she suspected this. She also debated where Cal Wayne fitted in the picture. He was surely a strange young man.

It seemed pointless to her that she and Monty had quarreled about her seeing Cal Wayne. And she decided she should go on into the lounge and try and talk to Monty and make this clear to him. She saw him as perhaps her staunchest friend at the hotel and she did not want to lose his support.

As usual the lounge was crowded. The head waiter found her a table near the door. It was a poor spot but the best available. She made sure that Monty had seen her before she sat down. His only recognition of her had been a solemn nod of his head as he went on playing.

She ordered a drink and waited for his break, thinking that he might come by her table and stop for a chat during his rest period. As it happened that was exactly what he did.

He came to her table with a glass in hand. 'Mind if I sit down?' he asked with formal politeness.

She smiled up at him. 'No. I've been hoping you'd come by.'

Monty sat and regarded her somewhat sheepishly. Then he said, 'I'm sorry I made such a fuss about you being with Cal Wayne.'

'It's all right.'

'I want to explain and apologize,' he said. 'It's just that Wayne is the kind of person I don't like. Saratoga gamblers aren't the nicest people you'll meet.'

'I know.'

'But you still saw him.'

'Because when you're dealing with the underworld it is often better to have one or two allies. Cal Wayne knows a lot of what is going on here.'

'I don't doubt that,' Monty said with a disgusted look at his glass. 'People of his type usually do.'

'I'm still hoping to find David Barry,' she reminded him.

'Must you?'

'It's why I came here.'

'Barry apparently doesn't want to be found.'

'Even so.'

'You ought to give up and get away from here,' Monty worried. 'Then you wouldn't be dealing with people like Cal Wayne. What has he to offer you?'

'Quite a bit of background facts. About Al Moroni for instance. According to Cal there's a reason for Moroni and his associates being at this hotel.'

'Oh? Did he tell you what reason?'

'No.'

'That doesn't help much,' Monty pointed out.

'No. But I feel Moroni being here may have something to do with David Barry.'

Monty groaned. 'We're back to him again. You'd have been better off if you'd never heard of him!'

'I'm sometimes inclined to think you're right,' she said with a sad smile.

'Well, then?'

'I won't give up now,' she said. 'The racing season only lasts about nine more days. I mean the main season. I'll have to stay that long and find out what I can.'

Monty gave her a worried appraisal. 'A lot can happen in nine days. In nine seconds for that matter! It wouldn't take much longer than a few seconds to get yourself murdered!'

'Please!'

'I think you should be realistic about this,' Monty warned her.

'You're being plain gruesome!'

'I'm worried about you,' he told her. 'I will be until you are out of this hotel.'

She looked at him seriously. 'Do you know something you haven't told me?'

'I know there have been two murders here in the past two years and I don't want to hear there is another. Especially not if the victim happens to be someone I care for a great deal.'

Andrea smiled at him. 'That's a nice thought. I've told you I promise to be careful.'

'Not enough,' he said.

She glanced at her watch. 'It's getting late. I'm going up to bed. It's been a long, exhausting day.'

'I have to return to the piano,' he said. 'Please do take care.'

'I feel very secure in the new room they've given me.'

'There's no place in this hotel you dare let yourself feel secure,' Monty warned.

They left the table and Monty went back to the piano while Andrea walked out to the lobby. She went over to the elevator and saw that there was no one in it. Grant was standing behind the desk with his back to her as he scanned some filing material. She knew if she decided to use the elevator she would have to ask him to man it since Olaf wasn't around. And she had no desire to be alone in the elevator with him after learning he could be the murderer.

She decided that instead she would use the stairs. It would take a little longer but she wouldn't have to deal with Grant. Having arrived at that decision she started up the stairway. She had barely reached the third floor when the lights suddenly went out. She halted and waited with her hand on the railing of the third floor landing.

Every so often the old hotel had fuses blow out. The wiring was old and not able to handle the heavy load of modern electrical equipment. For the most part it was a nuisance which only lasted a few minutes at most. But this was the first time she'd ever known the lights in the hallways to fail. And since it was now pitch dark it created a serious situation.

If any of the old people became restive and frightened in their rooms and came out into the strange darkness it could bring an added hazard of falls and other injuries. She stood patiently waiting and thinking how strange it was to be there in the dark. After several minutes she began to wonder if the power failure was only in the hotel or whether it extended to the entire area.

With a view to finding this out she groped her way to the landing windows and stared out. She could see the distant twinkling lights of the town and so this proved that the trouble was with the power in the hotel only. Again she groped her way back to the railing and took hold of it.

Now she began to feel uneasy as she waited there in the darkness. She could hear the sound of voices calling out to each other below and pictured the chaos this letting up of light would create even at this late hour when most of the regular guests were in bed. She'd noticed that in many of the public rooms there were emergency lamps on batteries in the corner which went on automatically when the regular lights failed. She wished they were on the stairways as well but seemingly they were not.

As the seconds went by her tension grew. All at once the darkness held menace for her and she wished fervently that she had at least reached the safety of her own room before the lights had all gone out. Memory of the terrifying experience she'd so recently gone through rose up in her mind and made her more nervous.

She was trembling and now she thought she heard someone on the stairs. She knew this was to be expected, that someone might have started up this way rather than wait for the elevator to work. The movement on the stairs came nearer.

'Someone there?' she called out nervously.

There was no reply. This was frightening in itself and more so when she heard a board of the landing creak only a short distance behind her. She wheeled around, crouching a little and feeling that she was being stalked!

'If anyone is there, please answer me!' she cried out in fear.

Again she received no reply. Now she was positive there was someone hovering close to her in the pitch blackness of the landing. Someone whose intent was violent. She could remain there no longer. Lights or no lights, she had to try and make her way to her own room on the floor above!

With this in mind she kept her hand on the railing and groped her way to the next stairway. She found the bannister and started up the stairs. She'd not gone three steps when she heard familiar heavy breathing from behind her and she knew! She knew it was the phantom killer of the other night breathing so hoarsely at her heels!

'No!' she screamed.

And in her panic she stumbled on the stairs. It was all the advantage her stalker needed. Almost at once she felt rough hands seize her. She struggled and tried to escape from them to no avail. And now once again she felt something being slipped around her throat. She tried to scream for help once more and couldn't.

The grip on her throat tightened and she was having a great deal of difficulty breathing. Her eyes were staring and she was gasping for breath. She struggled weakly but got nowhere. Then there was a burst of dazzling light! Light which seemed brighter than anything she'd known before! She saw it with a feeling of gratitude without really knowing why.

And with the coming of the light the tightness around her throat seemed to ease. She felt herself slumping down on the stairs as the hands which had held her captive released her. She lay there sobbing and mumbling words of thanks and fear, all so hopelessly mixed up that they made no sense.

There was a shadow over her and she cowed away from it. To her at this moment the shadow represented only a threat. Then her vision cleared and she saw that the shadow had a face. The face of Monty Freeman, the young pianist.

'Andrea!' Monty was calling out her name loudly. And his hands had gripped her shoulders. 'Andrea, speak to me!'

She stared up at him in disbelief. 'Monty!' she murmured.

'What happened? Did you fall down the stairs in the dark?' he wanted to know.

'The lights went out,' she said weakly.

'I know that,' he replied. 'And I guessed you

208

had started up the stairs on your own. What happened?'

'Someone came after me,' she managed.

His eyes widened. 'Came after you?'

She felt too weary to explain properly. 'The same as before. My neck! Tried to choke me!'

Monty was examining her neck now. 'You're right! I can see the mark of whatever it was! Did you see who it was when the lights came on?'

She shook her head hopelessly. 'No.'

'You saw nothing?'

'No.'

'That's great!' the young man said bitterly. 'Do you think you can get to your feet?'

'In a minute,' she said, her eyes half-closed. Now she was feeling

'Don't worry about it,' Monty said. 'I'll carry you.' And he lifted her in his arms and began carrying her up the stairs. He then took her down the hallway to the door of her own room, got the key from her and opened the door.

At last she was safely stretched out on her bed. She gave him a troubled look. 'You should be downstairs playing!'

'They can wait,' the young pianist said abruptly. 'I'm going to get you a strong brandy. It will bring you around.'

She nodded weakly and closed her eyes. She had no idea how long he was gone. Then she heard his voice and that of the manager's in troubled discussion. She raised her eyelids and saw they were entering her room together and Monty had the promised brandy with him.

Monty came and held it to her lips. She sat up in the bed and sipped the fiery amber liquid. 'Better,' she murmured.

Ernest Clayton stood by her bedside in almost comic frustration. He demanded of Monty, 'How did you come to be on the stairs?'

Monty turned to him with annoyance. 'I realized she had either taken the elevator or started up the stairs. When the elevator was still there I tried the stairs. I was worried about her being alone in the darkness.'

'You'd left the lounge?'

'Yes. No one was listening to me anyway,' Monty said with a touch of anger. 'They were all upset about the lights going out.'

'Didn't the emergency lights go on in the lounge?'

'Yes,' Monty said. 'But everyone knew the regular lights were out.'

As she finished the balance of the brandy the hotel manager gave her a troubled glance and then said to Monty, 'So by the time you'd reached Miss Gibbs the lights had come on again.'

'Yes.'

'And you found her on the stairs complaining of another attack on her?'

'I've already told you that,' Monty said to the little man in a tone of exasperation.

Andrea now felt able to speak up. She said, 'Everything he's told you is correct.'

'Thank you,' the manager said. 'This is a dreadful business. I don't know what caused the fuses to go this time but the whole building was involved. I don't think that has ever happened before.'

'I don't remember it,' Monty said.

From her bed Andrea said, 'Giving the silk-stocking murderer an ideal opportunity to strike at me again.'

The manager looked stunned. He asked her, 'Who saw you starting up the stairs before the lights went out?'

'I don't know,' she said. 'Grant was at the desk. He could well have seen me.'

The manager nodded grimly. 'Grant!'

'Yes,' she said, knowing what he must be thinking since he already suspected Grant. 'And I suppose Monty knew it. He guessed I'd used the stairs and was able to find me.'

'Who else?' the manager wanted to know.

'I haven't any idea,' she said.

The manager scowled. 'Whoever followed you and tried to attack you knew you would be on the stairs. So they must have seen you start up them.'

'That sounds reasonable,' she agreed.

'But you didn't have to have seen them,' the manager said. 'It is all very confusing.'

Monty Freeman gave him a knowing look. 'I'd say that this time the police should be

211

notified.'

The manager raised a stubby-fingered hand. 'Don't try to tell me what I should do.'

'Reason demands it!' Monty argued.

'I don't know,' the manager said in a distressed way. 'Once again we have so little to work on. Even less than last time. Don't you agree, Miss Gibbs?'

'We haven't much to go on,' she admitted.

Monty Freeman looked from her to the manager and said, 'I don't see how you can allow this to go on without reporting it!'

'Let me handle it my way,' the manager pleaded. 'I can spare the hotel needless notoriety and still gain some help from the local police.'

'How?' Monty demanded.

'I have a friend on the local police force,' Ernest Clayton went on. 'His name is Inspector Magee. I'll get in touch with him privately and tell him what has been going on here and get his advice.'

'Can you manage that?' Monty asked.

'Yes. I've had to turn to him for help before. We had several robbery cases and he proved most helpful.'

'There is a difference,' Monty reminded him. 'This time you're dealing with attempted murder!'

'I can depend on him,' the manager insisted.

Andrea had been dodging the argument between the two men but now she felt she should try to placate them. She said, 'I think what Mr. Clayton suggests is logical and I think he should be allowed to try it.'

'Thank you, Miss Gibbs,' the manager said and he gave Monty a condescending smile. 'I'm sure it's the better way to take care of this.'

'We'll see,' was Monty's dry comment.

'You should return to the lounge,' the manager told Monty. 'And I must go down and find out what really happened and what Olaf did to fix the lights and get them going again.'

The little man left them. When they were alone Monty gave her a pleading look. 'Well, didn't this convince you that you're really in danger?'

'I've guessed that all along.'

'And you don't care?'

'I wouldn't say that,' she told him.

'But you're not leaving?'

'No. I still want to find David Barry.'

Monty gave her a significant glance. 'Maybe the police will have something to say about that.'

She frowned. 'What do you mean?'

'I don't know. Nothing, I guess. It was something to say.'

Andrea didn't believe this. She was certain he'd had something in mind when he said it and was now not willing to admit it. She told him, 'You'd better get back to your piano in the lounge or Mr. Clayton will be discharging you.'

'That might be a break for me,' the young man said, in a disgruntled tone.

'Please, for me,' she begged him. And she got up from the bed. Standing before him, she told him, 'I do appreciate what you did for me. You helped save my life.'

'I can't take any credit,' he complained. 'There was no one in sight but you when I got there. You were stretched out on the steps as if in a faint.

'Whoever it was scurried off at the first hint of the lights coming on.'

'Or vanished into thin air,' he said unhappily. 'Maybe we are dealing with a ghost.'

She sighed. 'There are times when you'd believe it.' And she raised her lips to be kissed. He responded and held her in his arms for a moment. When he let her go, she said softly, 'Thank you, Monty; that helped.'

He stared at her in despair. 'Now you expect me to go back down to the piano?'

She managed a smile and turned him around and marched him to the door. 'Please, go,' she said.

As he stepped outside Edna came by. The little woman halted and studied them with a smile. She said, 'Well, I hear there has been lots of excitement around here tonight.'

'There has,' Monty agreed.

Edna told him, 'They were asking for you in

the lobby when I came through. I think the head waiter in the lounge wants you.'

'I'm on my way!' Monty replied and hurried off to the stairs and down.

Edna smiled at her. 'Where were you when the lights failed?'

'On the stairs. I had a fright. Monty came to make sure I was all right,' she said, not feeling free to tell the pleasant Edna more than that at the moment.

'I was out to the trotting races on Nelson Avenue,' Edna said. 'I go every so often.'

'You're a racing fan!'

Edna laughed, her blue eyes bright. 'I won twenty-five dollars tonight. That's not bad.'

'You did very well,' Andrea said. 'Who was in the lobby that we know when you came through?'

'You'll never believe it but old Mrs. Flanders was down there,' Edna told her. 'Wouldn't stay in her dark room alone. It's a wonder she didn't break a leg getting down to the lobby. She's over sixty and uses a cane.'

'She did take a chance! Anyone else?'

Edna considered. 'Yes. That awful-looking Moroni man was there by the newsstand and he had that girl with him. And your friend was there.'

'My friend?' she questioned the older woman in a puzzled tone.

'I was just joking,' Edna said. 'I mean Cal Wayne. The fellow with the dark glasses. First

215

time I've seen him in the lobby for ages.'

'He was there?' she asked faintly.

'Yes.'

'I see,' she said. 'Well, he is staying here.' These were mere words to hide what she was really thinking. If Cal Wayne had been in the hotel it was possible it was he who'd made the attack on her and the previous one as well.

Edna studied her. 'You look weary,' the white-haired woman said. 'I'm talking too much. I'll see you tomorrow.'

'Yes, tomorrow,' she said, still stunned by what she'd heard and the meaning she'd taken from it. 'Goodnight.' She went inside and locked her door.

She recalled that the manager of the hotel had complained that all the door locks were old fashioned and too easy to open. The ancient building with its weak lighting system and almost total lack of security wasn't a safe place to be. No wonder Monty wanted her to leave.

She began changing into her night clothes. She was feeling the strain of this latest attack on her and by the time she slipped between the cold bed sheets she felt that she would quickly be able to sleep. But after she'd turned off the lights she remained awake with her heart pounding.

It had been a grim evening for her. And now she was feeling the results of it. She could only hope that Ernest Clayton's friend in the

216

local police department might come up with something helpful.

At the moment the question that concerned her most was, what about Cal Wayne? He had continually tried to make her suspicious of Monty Freeman, pointing out rightly that she knew nothing at all about the background of the young pianist. But probably he'd done this as a clever ruse to keep her from pressing for more information about him.

She could not help but believe that Cal was the more likely of the two to be a psychotic killer. There was a tenseness about him all the time which she had observed. Yet, was it fair to at once think of him as her attacker because he happened to be in the hotel when it happened?

Grant had been there also. She'd seen him at the desk and it was quite likely he'd gotten a glimpse of her as she'd started up the stairs. And how easy it would have been for him to follow her when the lights went out? And the heavy breathing suggested an older man to whom attacking her was an effort managed only by mad strength! Grant whom the manager felt might have been the original silk-stocking murderer!

The more she thought about it the more she was convinced that it might have well been Grant. She would have to talk to Ernest Clayton about this in the morning. Perhaps his police officer friend would cautiously query

Grant and see if the old man said anything to give himself away.

A knock on the door broke into Andrea's reverie. She at once sat up in bed with a frightened expression on her pretty face. 'Yes?' she called out.

'Are you all right?' a familiar sing-song voice inquired. 'This is Olaf.'

She felt a great surge of relief. 'Yes! Yes, thank you, Olaf. I'm fine. Glad to know you're making your rounds.'

'Every night, Miss,' the man on the other side of the door assured her. 'I was kept late tonight by the lights going out. I had to go down to the cellar to take care of them.'

'What happened?'

'I don't know, Miss,' the old man said. 'It seems someone tampered with the main switch. It threw everything out at once. Goodnight, Miss.'

'Goodnight,' she said. And she still sat up in bed as she listened to the night watchman's heavy steps as they faded down the corridor. So someone had tampered with the main switch! Perhaps purposely to make the attack on her easier. It sounded like the work of a madman.

She sank back on her pillow and closed her eyes. She was too weary to think it out now. Almost at once she fell asleep. She was awakened by the phone ringing furiously and sat up. It was dark but she had no idea what time it was. Trembling she reached for the phone.

CHAPTER TEN

The moment she picked up the phone a muffled voice which was by now familiar to her, said, 'I suppose you didn't expect to hear from me again.'

Tensely, she asked, 'Is that you, David?'

'Who else?' There was a chuckle from the other end of the line.

'You know I was told you were dead.'

'I'm very much alive,' the muffled voice informed her. 'But you could be dead. I hope you realize that.'

'I know,' she said. 'I've been attacked twice.'

'And you still insist on remaining in that hotel and in Saratoga?'

'I won't leave until I meet you,' she told him.

'That presents a problem,' the muffled voice said. 'For various reasons it is difficult for me to arrange a meeting with you.'

'Why?'

'I can't tell you now.'

'There must be a way,' she insisted.

'Perhaps if we met in some isolated place after dark,' he said. 'There are some old stables at the rear of the Ansonia. Beyond the shuffleboard area. Suppose you meet me there tomorrow night at ten o'clock.'

'Ten o'clock,' she said. 'I'll be there.'

'I'll expect you to show yourself first,' he warned her. 'I'll be watching. And when I'm sure it is safe I'll come out and join you.'

'What are you so afraid of?'

'I'll have to explain that later,' the muffled voice told her. 'Be careful that you aren't followed.'

'The hotel grounds can be dangerous,' she said. 'But I'll know you'll be out there so I won't be afraid.'

'I wouldn't ask you to meet me if I didn't feel I could protect you,' the voice said.

'I do want to meet you, David,' she said earnestly. 'I'd like to have some understanding with you and then get away from here.'

'I would have preferred that you leave at once,' David Barry said. 'But since you won't be persuaded without a meeting I'll see you tomorrow night.'

'Then you can tell me why you've behaved this way,' she said.

'Don't expect all the answers,' he warned her. 'Some things must wait.'

'Very well,' she said. 'Tomorrow at ten by the stables in the rear of the hotel.'

'Yes,' he said. And then he hung up and the line returned to a dial tone.

She put the phone down with mixed feelings. She was pleased to have received the call and the promise of a meeting with David. But she also worried about whether the call was genuine. Had she really talked to David or had she been in conversation with the mad murderer ready to lure her into a trap? It was a troublesome question.

Her head on her pillow she stared up into the darkness and tried to think what she should do. The voice on the phone had warned her not to tell anyone else of the meeting. If she followed these instructions she would have to face the danger alone.

She finally had a fairly decent sleep and woke up the next morning to find that it was raining. A rainy day meant there would be no races and as a result the hotel would be busier all through the day. The lounge generally was filled only at night but on rainy days it did a roaring business.

She went down and had breakfast at the staff table in the dining room. Ernest Clayton was also there and she sat next to him deliberately. The stout man seemed in an aloof, troubled mood.

She at once told him, 'I've been thinking about last night. I'm almost sure Grant saw me starting upstairs. I think you should have your police officer friend question him.'

The manager eyed her nervously. 'You think so?'

'I do.'

'Very well,' he said. 'I'll see that it's done. But don't expect immediate results. These things are managed slowly.'

She was surprised that he had seemingly lost

much of his enthusiasm of the previous night. She said, 'You must make a determined effort to find out who has been attacking me. As long as that madman is at large the hotel is in danger of being involved in another scandal.'

'True,' he said grimly. 'I'm fully aware of that. And what you say about Grant may be the answer to the whole problem.'

'You probably feel badly about having to put the law on someone who has been associated with you for so long,' she said, in an effort to test his frame of mind.

'That is so,' he agreed. 'But if Grant is the guilty party his paying for his crimes must be considered long overdue. We will have to proceed and find out the truth if we can.'

'I agree,' she replied.

The manager finished his breakfast first and left her alone at the staff table. After awhile Edna came and sat down with her.

The white-haired woman said, 'We can count on a heavy lunch-hour business with this rain.'

'When is it supposed to let up?'

'Clearing by six,' Edna said with a sigh. 'That means there won't be any racing today.'

'There have been only a few wet days.'

'Luckily. The law requires there be twenty-one racing days at the big track. So the weather has to be pretty fair or it drags on.'

'I'll come in a few minutes early,' Andrea promised.

'No need of that,' Edna said. 'I can handle things until you arrive.'

After breakfast she went out into the lobby and almost the first person to greet her was Al Moroni. The swarthy gangster seemed in an especially good mood. He said, 'You look beautiful this morning.'

'Thank you,' she said with cool politeness. 'It is a nasty day.'

He eyed her with what seemed inner amusement. And he said, 'I don't know. Maybe it's a bad day for some but I'm satisfied.'

She arched an eyebrow. 'You don't mind losing a racing day?'

'No,' he said. 'I don't mind. I've got other things which interest me as much as the horses.'

'Really?'

He nodded. 'Sure. Pretty girls for one!'

She felt the conversation was getting embarrassing. So she said pointedly, 'Your wife is very attractive.'

He raised his eyebrows. 'Rose?'

'Yes.'

'She ain't my wife,' he said.

'Oh! I'm sorry. I'd assumed that she was.'

Moroni laughed scornfully. 'You assumed wrong. She's a girlfriend of mine. Sure she's pretty but she doesn't have your class. What I really appreciate is a girl with class!'

She said, 'You'll excuse me. There's

someone standing by the lounge entrance I must talk to.'

Al Moroni glanced in the direction of the lounge entrance to see Monty Freeman standing there. He said with disgust, 'That piano player? They come a dime a dozen. He won't do you any good.'

Andrea didn't wait to answer him. She was already on her way across the lobby to greet Monty who was standing awaiting her arrival with a look of grim humor on his pleasant face.

When she came up to him, she said, 'I've just escaped a bothersome situation.'

'Moroni?'

'Yes.' She grimaced.

He eyed her with a smile. 'I thought you two were hitting it off great. You were having quite a conversation.'

'He was holding me there against my will,' she asserted.

'Didn't look that way.'

'I'm sorry.'

Monty said, 'What do you think of the day?'

'Terrible,' she told him. 'I have a bad leg. I broke it in a couple of places when I was skiing last year. On a day like this it aches.'

'You're like the rest of the old ladies around here,' he teased her. 'A bundle of aches and pains.'

'I'm not all that bad,' she said.

'Clayton has asked me to play in the lounge after lunch,' Monty said with disgust. 'I guess

225

he figures on a big day in there.'

'It is usually crowded on rainy days,' she agreed.

'What are you going to do?'

'I don't know,' she said. 'Sleep maybe. I didn't do too well in the sleep department last night.'

Monty gave her a sharp look. 'Did you have a talk with Clayton about bringing that police officer in? You said you'd mention it to him again this morning.'

'I have. But he seems evasive.'

'I've noticed that,' Monty said grimly. 'After I came down here last night I had a thought. He's always telling about Grant being here at the time that first girl was murdered years ago, but he doesn't say much about the fact he was here as well.'

She gave the pianist a surprised look. 'You're right.'

Monty went on, 'I don't know any reason why Clayton couldn't have been mixed up in that first murder. And he was here when the others were committed.'

'Yes,' she said somewhat stunned that she hadn't thought of this before. But Ernest Clayton had seemed above suspicion. Yet was he?

'So he could have good reasons for not wanting the murderer found. He could be the madman.'

Thinking aloud, she said, 'And he has that

strange friendship with Catherine Flanders!'

'What's that?' the pianist asked.

'I was talking to myself. It wasn't important,' she told him almost too quickly.

He studied her with suspicion. 'Well, what do you say to my latest theory?'

'You've had quite a few.'

'This could be the important one.'

'I'll need to think about it,' she said. 'Ernest Clayton doesn't strike me as a person who could murder.'

'He could be just the type,' Monty warned her.

'I'll keep it in mind. And he'll bring suspicion on himself if he doesn't go through with calling in that policeman friend of his.'

Monty nodded. 'If he stalls on that I'll be thinking more about him as the possible guilty one than I will of Grant.'

'And Ernest Clayton was also in the hotel last night. So he could have made the attack on me. Whoever it was breathed heavily as if the effort were a great strain.'

'Clayton is fat and short of breath.'

'Let's stop it,' she protested. 'Otherwise we'll be convicting him in our minds and we may be all wrong.'

'Possibly. I'm not so sure.'

'The trouble is,' she reminded him, 'we're not sure about anything yet.'

'All too true,' he agreed.

Still the talk remained with her and all

through the lunch period she wondered about it. If Ernest Clayton were the murderer they'd been playing into his hands. They'd told him every move they were making and every suspicion they had in advance. She didn't think the hotel manager could be guilty of the long ago murder and the two recent ones, yet there was a slim chance she was wrong.

The dining room was filled at lunch time. The elderly regulars were jostled about by the heavy transient trade and not happy about the situation. Several of them complained to Andrea and she had to agree that their complaints were justified.

Toward the end of the lunch period Al Moroni, Jake Gotell and Rose came into the dining room. All three of them seemed in special good humor as if they shared some private joke. Andrea found herself wondering what it was all about.

Edna took over for the last fifteen minutes completely which gave Andrea a chance to sit down to her own lunch before it became too late. She ate lightly, her mind full of troubling questions. At least one thing was in her favor. The weather was supposed to clear at six so with any luck she'd have no problem meeting David Barry at ten o'clock.

Thoughts of at last meeting the elusive newspaperman cheered her. She had grimly stayed on in Saratoga despite all the dangers she'd undergone and the hazards she still faced. And her reward was that she'd finally won a promise from David to meet her. But then he'd promised to meet her once before in New York City and hadn't appeared. But she thought he would show up this time. She was counting on it. Counting on his being out there to protect her.

When she left the dining room after lunch she had a sudden compulsion to see and talk with the odd Catherine Flanders once again. She had no idea whether the eccentric woman would see her or not but she felt it was worth a try. She went upstairs to the door of the suite and knocked.

The maid came and peered out at her. 'Yes?'

'May I speak with Mrs. Flanders for a moment?' she asked.

'Is she expecting you?'

'No.'

'Then I'm afraid not. Madame only sees callers by special appointment,' the maid said nervously and appeared ready to close the door in Andrea's face.

'I'd only take a few minutes of her time,' she protested.

Just then the voice of Catherine Flanders could be heard in the background as she called out to the maid. 'Who is that?'

The maid turned and informed her, 'It's that Miss Gibbs who was here last night.'

'Send her in to me,' the distant voice

ordered the maid with authority.

Looking forlorn the elderly woman said to Andrea, 'You can come in.' And she opened the door for her. 'You know where to find her.'

'Thank you,' Andrea said. She entered the dark apartment and made her way through the eerie shadows to the small study. And she found her seated there above the glowing crystal ball. The weird light from the crystal ball gave her emaciated face a ghostly look. She smiled for Andrea's benefit.

Gesturing to the chair across from her with a thin hand the woman in black intoned, 'Do sit down.'

Rather nervously Andrea took the offered chair. As she sat in it she studied the white, thin face of Catherine Flanders, noting the dark shadows under the woman's eyes and the gray hollows of her cheeks.

'You have come at a good time,' the demented woman informed her.

'Have I?'

'Yes. Just a few minutes ago I clearly saw a face from the past in the crystal. A face known years ago in this hotel. The face of the girl who was murdered. She looked up at me and seemed to want to tell me something and then she just faded away.'

Andrea felt a chill run down her spine. She said, 'What could she have wanted to say to you?'

The pale face showed a wary smile. 'I think

I know.'

'What?'

'The name of the man who murdered her,' Catherine Flanders said triumphantly. 'One day she'll appear in my crystal again and tell me. And then James will come to me in the crystal and we shall be reunited.'

Andrea said, 'You're sure she didn't tell you the name of her killer just now?'

'No,' the woman in black shook her head. 'She told me nothing. But she did look up at me and seem about to speak. It is one of my good psychic days. Many dead faces have shown themselves to me.'

'But the killer must still be living,' Andrea suggested.

This didn't go down well with the woman in black. 'No!' she said sharply as they sat there in the near darkness. 'They are all dead. Everyone's dead but me! I have fooled them!'

There was something strange and frightening in the thin woman's high-pitched declaration. Andrea sat there feeling a definite revulsion for her but still perversely fascinated by her.

Quietly she said, 'They are not all dead. Grant is still alive. You remember Grant?'

Catherine Flanders sat silently for a moment and then the shadow of a sad smile crossed her ruined face. In a trance-like state, she said, 'Yes, I remember Grant. Of course I do. We had wonderful parties in the ballroom.

Grant was always there! The waltzes! He was a fine waltzer! And he always chose me first for his partner!'

She said, 'Yes. That was Grant. He was the social director.'

'Handsome!' the woman in black informed her. 'Grant was handsome. We were all half in love with him.'

Andrea said, 'He's not very handsome today. But he's still alive. He works as night clerk. His health is bad and he drinks too much.'

Catherine Flanders was paying no attention to her. Lost in the past, she went on, 'One night I was dancing with Grant and we waltzed right out onto the verandah. Then he kissed me. It was a daring thing to do. And I responded. I was starved for love. And then he stepped out of the shadows and we were both frightened.'

Andrea was caught up in the story. 'Who?' she asked tautly. 'Who came out of the shadows?'

'Ernest Clayton,' the woman in black said.

'What did he say?'

'He took Grant aside and spoke quickly to him,' Catherine Flanders said. 'Then he let him take me back into the ballroom. But Grant never asked me to dance with him again. I hated Ernest Clayton for that!'

She was astounded by the amount of venom in the other woman's voice. She said, 'What then?'

'It was the beginning of my seeing Ernest Clayton,' the woman in black said. 'At the start I hated him. But he has always held a kind of strange power over me. He's an odd little man but there is something about his eyes. Have you ever looked straight into his eyes?'

'No.'

'You must. There is a strange lost world in those eyes. Only by peering into them can you see it. Ernest is cruel and yet he can be kind. I have grown to depend on him. Now you might say I'm almost at his mercy. I shall never be free of him.'

'Are you saying he is evil?'

'In his way.'

'What about James Dennis?' Andrea asked tensely. 'How did Ernest Clayton feel about him?'

'He wanted James Dennis to die. He wanted that as soon as he learned Dennis and I were lovers. He hated anyone who loved me.'

'Would you say he hated enough to kill?'

The woman in black seemed to come out of her spell. Now she looked at her oddly. 'What have we been talking about?'

'The old days. Ernest Clayton and what you think of him.'

'No!' the woman's pale face showed terror. 'I didn't tell you anything! I couldn't have! I have never said a word against Ernest. He is the only one now! The only one who truly

233

loves me!'

'He seems to know more about hate than love,' Andrea said, thinking she might get the old woman back on her previous line of thought again.

But it was not to be. Catherine Flanders had gotten to her feet. 'You must go now,' she said. 'I cannot talk to you any longer.'

Andrea rose. 'Please,' she said. 'I have only just arrived.'

'No. You have stayed too long! Go!'

She saw there was nothing for it but to leave. Hesitating, she told the woman in black, 'I hope I may return again.'

'I make no promises,' the demented woman said.

So she left the shadowed apartment with its glowing crystal ball and all those ghosts from the past. She hadn't learned much, but she had gained a little.

It seemed impossible that the stout little bald man whom she'd met as the present manager of the hotel had ever been such an ardent Romeo. It appeared that he still held a strange control over Catherine Flanders. Certainly she feared him. Why?

The murder of that girl and James Dennis being blamed for it must have seemed like the best of luck to Ernest Clayton at the time. He could not know then that shortly Catherine Flanders would have a breakdown which would leave her a broken woman impossible to love as he had loved her in the old days. Fate had played a wry trick on him and he'd wound up as the protector of the distraught woman.

But had he killed for her? That was the question which plagued Andrea. It was one that she must find the answer to though she had no idea how, at the moment.

It was still raining and she went up to her room to have a nap. She'd barely stretched out on the bed when the phone rang and she gave a small groan and reached out to pick it up.

'Yes,' she said, to what seemed like a silent line.

Then a frightened female voice asked, 'Is that Miss Gibbs? Andrea Gibbs?'

'It is,' she said. 'Who is this?'

'Don't you recognize my voice?'

'No.'

'It's Bertha!'

For a moment it didn't jibe in her memory. She said, 'Bertha, who?'

'Bertha Walsh! Remember? You came to see me about my cousin?'

'Yes,' she said, wearily. 'Now I remember.'

'I told you I would call.'

'Did you?' Andrea was wary of the woman whom she'd been told was a drug addict.

'Yes. I said I'd phone you if I found out anything that could help you.'

'Go on,' she said.

'Well, I've found out something.'

'What?'

'I can't tell you on the phone,' the nervous Bertha almost wailed.

Holding the phone Andrea glanced at the window with the rain streaming down its panes. She said, 'Why not?'

'It wouldn't do,' Bertha said.

'So?'

'I want you to come here to my place,' Bertha said.

'It's raining.'

'What does that matter?' the nervous woman exploded angrily.

'Is what you have to tell me really important?'

'Yes. I wouldn't have called you otherwise!'

'I see,' she said with a sigh. 'Are you at home now?'

'Yes. Can you come right away?' There was urgency in the woman's voice.

'All right,' she said wearily. 'But I warn you this had better not be a wild goose chase.'

'This is on the level. I swear it!' Bertha said.

She felt that Bertha would swear to anything now that she'd been left alone. She needed money for dope and the only hope was that she might have some information worth the money Andrea knew she would undoubtedly have to pay for it.

She put on her raincoat and hat and boots and then went out to the car. The rain had slacked a trifle in view of the promise it would be clear by early evening. Andrea knew the way this time and drove straight to the corner where the drugstore was located. Finding a parking place for her car near the corner she dodged through the rain and entered the door leading to the dark, smelly stairway.

She knocked on the door of the apartment. The same procedure as before was repeated with Bertha Walsh opening the door on its chain and shakily inquiring who she was. She told her and she let her in. She was dressed in the same housecoat as before and seemed in the identical weird state. She might never have left her.

The pinched-faced Bertha stood before her nervously. She was wearing the usual over-size pale blue sunglasses. She said, 'I was afraid you weren't coming.'

'I said I'd be here,' she reminded her.

'Sure,' the thin woman said. 'Could you use a drink?'

'All right. Where?'

'I've got booze right here. We don't need to go nowhere,' the pale Bertha said nervously. 'You like Scotch?'

'Yes.'

'How?'

'Some ice and water,' she said.

Bertha went to the kitchen and spent an inordinately long time getting the simple drink. She brought it back to Andrea with the air of somebody who'd accomplished something.

Andrea took the drink. 'What about you?'

'I don't use it,' the henna-haired one said emphatically.

She recalled being told that most drug addicts don't have a taste for alcohol. But she pretended to feel hurt. 'You expect me to drink alone?'

'Yes. I have some information for you. But it is going to cost you money.'

'I expected that.'

'I'm not well,' Bertha said. 'I have to pick up my dollars where I can.'

'How many do you plan to pick up this time?' she asked.

The woman looked around nervously. 'What I have to tell you should be worth fifty. I'm taking a big chance having you here.'

'It's about David Barry? Not your cousin. The real David Barry?'

'Yes,' Bertha nodded excitedly.

'All right,' she said. And she took two twenties and a ten from her purse and gave them to the bedraggled Bertha.

'I'm giving you a bargain,' Bertha promised as she quickly stuffed the money in the pocket of her housecoat.

'Don't keep me in suspense,' she said, sipping her drink.

Bertha stood before her nervously. 'This ain't easy for me. I don't make a practice of being a stool pigeon.'

'I'm not impressed,' she said. 'Get on with

it.'

'You knew about my cousin, David Barry.'

'Yes.'

'Well, before they killed him he came around here one night. He used to like to come by and talk with me. He said I was the only one left who had known his father and mother. Often he wanted to talk of nothing but the old days. That's what gave me the idea of this being a good time to return to the old country while a few of my people are still alive.'

'You'll make it,' Andrea said.

'I don't know. I don't count on it,' the little woman said. 'Well, this night he came and talked to me and he said would you believe it, I have a double right here in Saratoga. He has a name like me but he doesn't look anything like me and he's a lot younger.'

'How did your cousin know about my David Barry?' she asked.

The woman went on. 'According to him they met over at that motel Nick Lucas runs. He thought it was a big joke. He said this David Barry was young and good-looking and he was hooked on gambling.'

'Did your cousin learn why my David Barry had come to Saratoga?' Andrea asked.

Bertha's face showed a blank. 'No,' she said. 'I guess maybe the young guy came here to gamble. That would be enough.'

'What more did you learn about David

239

Barry?'

Bertha looked sly. 'Not much.'

Andrea put her drink aside. 'I'm not paying you any more money today,' she warned the woman. 'So you'd do well to remember and send me away a satisfied customer.'

'I was going to tell you,' the thin woman said defensively. 'Just give me time.'

'Take as long as you like.'

'If they find out I talked they'll kill me!'

'I doubt that!'

'They have killed people! Lots of people!'

'They'd better not try it on you at this point,' Andrea said. 'There is still some law in this country.'

'Not that touches them,' the woman said miserably.

'The law should count with everyone,' she said. 'I want to hear whatever you found out.'

'My cousin told me that your David Barry was a good friend of Slim Gordon, the jockey.'

'So that was how they met,' she said.

'What?' Bertha stared at her from behind the blue glasses with an air of fright.

'No need to be afraid,' Andrea said.

Bertha looked unconvinced. She said, 'So anyway that is somebody still living who knows David Barry.'

'Slim Gordon.'

'Yes.'

'I've met him at the Ansonia,' Andrea said. 'He's a thin little man.'

'Jockeys all are!'

'He was friendly with another man at the hotel, a Cal Wayne. Did you ever hear of him?'

Bertha shook her head. 'No.'

'Well, that's where I saw Slim Gordon. With this Wayne.'

Bertha said, 'You'd better go now. That's all I have to tell you.'

'Nothing more?'

'No.'

'You'll phone me again if you find anything else out?'

Bertha nodded. 'Sure.'

'I'll always be willing to pay you well,' she said. 'In fact I have another twenty which I'd turn over to you now if you could tell me where I can locate this Slim Gordon right away.'

The eyes behind the blue glasses blinked nervously. Then the henna-haired one reached out a thin hand. 'Give it to me.'

'Remember. I'll be back if what you tell me isn't true,' she warned the shaken woman.

Bertha said, 'You can depend on me.'

She took the twenty from her purse and gave it to her. 'It's the last of my cash so you may as well cooperate with me honestly,' she said.

'I never stole from anybody,' Bertha pouted.

'So don't begin with me now,' she said.

The woman in the housecoat twitched nervously. 'You want me to tell you where you can find Slim Gordon now?'

'Yes.'

'You know where the big race track is?'

'On Union Avenue.'

'That's it,' Bertha said. 'You go straight to the tracks. They've got a lot of stable buildings there. And today all the jockeys and so on will be inside the stables. You look for the one belonging to Hiram Johnson. That's who Gordon is riding for now.'

'You think he'll be there?'

'If he isn't he won't be far away. They'll tell you where to find him.'

Andrea sighed. 'I hope you're right.'

'I gave you my word.'

Andrea started out of the dingy apartment then she turned to ask the woman, 'Think hard. Did your cousin tell you anything about this other David Barry? Did he say anything about what he looked like?'

Bertha hesitated. 'I don't think so.' Then seeming to remember, she said, 'He did say that little punk isn't half my size and he doesn't have half my brains.'

'How large was your cousin?'

'He was a big man. Weighed almost two hundred and fifty pounds and he was near six feet.'

'That's all he said?'

'That's all,' the henna-haired woman said.

She left the apartment and went down the dark stairs and into the street. For just a moment she thought she'd come close to learning something about David Barry. But it had ended in failure. Or it would be a failure if the tip about jockey, Slim Gordon, didn't turn out to have any value. She wasn't sure Gordon would talk to her but she would drive out to the track and try and find him. And so she hurried across the street in the rain and slid behind the wheel of her car again.

CHAPTER ELEVEN

The rain was already beginning to ease as she neared the big Saratoga Raceway. It was a much different place on this wet day than when the weather was fine and the track was in full activity. But as she headed her car into the parking lot she saw there were a good many cars parked there. The behind-the-scenes business of buying and selling thoroughbreds, and the problems of training and preparing for the races went on no matter what the weather might be like.

She left her car and walking in the drizzle proceeded in the direction of the stables. She felt definitely self-conscious about her mission but she could not turn back now. Bertha had established that there was another David Barry in Saratoga and that he knew Slim Gordon. She felt she must follow this up.

She met a stableman leading a dappled, spirited thoroughbred with a colorful blanket thrown over it. She halted to ask where the Hiram Johnson stables were. The man paused to point the area out to her as he coped with the restless horse at the same time.

Andrea walked on until she reached the Johnson stables. And standing in the open doorway was the thin little jockey in conversation with a stout man in work clothes.

She managed to get right up to them before Slim Gordon realized she was there.

Quickly, she said, 'Could I speak with you a moment?'

The long, gloomy face of the little man took on a sullen shadow. 'I'm busy,' he told her.

'I won't keep you long,' she promised.

The stout man with the jockey gave her a curious glance and told the little man, 'I'll see you later, Slim.' And he walked away.

She moved inside the shelter of the doorway and now she could smell the pungent odor of the horses, wet blankets and hay. She faced the uneasy Slim Gordon, saying, 'I guess you must remember me. I'm the hostess in the dining room at the Ansonia Hotel.'

The little man showed a belligerent front. 'I remember you all right,' he said. 'So what do you want?'

'I need some information.'

'That's not my department,' the jockey said.

'I think it is in this case,' she said. 'You needn't worry about anything you should tell me. It's a purely personal matter. I'm looking for David Barry.'

The jockey's long face took on a frown. 'Barry is dead. He was knocked down by a hit-and-run driver.'

She shook her head. 'No.'

'That's what happened to him,' Slim Gordon said stubbornly.

'What about the other David Barry?'

245

He stared at her. 'Are you nuts?'

'No. I happen to be sure there is another David Barry in Saratoga. A newspaperman. And he's a friend of yours, I've been told.'

Now the jockey looked frightened. 'Somebody has been putting you on,' he said. 'There's no other David Barry here.'

'He could be calling himself by another name but he is here,' she said. 'And I've had it on good authority he's a friend of yours.'

'Who said that?' Slim Gordon asked in an upset voice.

'The dead David Barry told a friend of mine,' she said.

The jockey's lips were working nervously. He said, 'You're making that up!'

'Why should I?'

'Because nobody can prove what a dead man said.'

'I'm sure he knew what he was talking about,' she told Slim Gordon. 'And I guess there is some sort of trouble in which the other David Barry has a part. But I mean him no harm. I'm going to see him tonight. We have an appointment.'

He eyed her with disbelief. 'Then why come bothering me?'

'Because I'd like to know more about him before I keep that appointment,' she said. 'You've met him. You can tell me what he's like and why he's gone into hiding here.'

Slim Gordon said, 'Why don't you ask Cal

Wayne?'

'I have and he hasn't helped me.'

'Then don't expect anything from me,' the jockey warned her. 'Cal knows Barry better than I do. And he can tell you more about him.'

'I'm sure he won't.'

'Then that's your hard luck, lady,' Slim Gordon said with a nasty grin. 'I've got to be going. I have things to do.'

'You won't tell me anything?'

'I don't have anything to tell,' was the jockey's reply.

She sighed. 'Where would Cal Wayne be today?'

'Probably in a poker game at the Steeplechase motel or some other place like it,' the jockey said with a sour smile on his long face. 'I ain't his guardian, lady. I don't know where he spends his spare time.'

'Thanks!' she said, bitterly.

'You're much obliged,' the jockey said mockingly and he left her and vanished in the shadows of the stable.

Andrea walked back to the parking lot feeling humiliated. She'd not expected too much from the jockey but he'd turned out even tougher than she'd anticipated. But after she got into her car and began the drive back to the Ansonia she began to review her conversation with Slim Gordon and decided she had gained at least one point. He had definitely stated that Cal Wayne knew David Barry better than he did. So this left Cal as her most direct link with the elusive Barry. But Cal had refused to help her. Why? She was beginning to suspect that for some reason he was an enemy of David Barry's.

If she saw Cal Wayne before her rendezvous with David Barry at ten o'clock that night she would try and get some information from him about Barry. In the meantime all she could do was wait.

By the time she reached the hotel it was getting near six and the sun had come out. The weatherman's prediction had been right for once. She hurried inside and up to her room. She showered and changed into a gown of pale yellow for her chores in the dining room.

Edna was waiting for her in the entrance to the dining room. The thin little woman had on her usual neat white uniform and had some menus in hand. She told Andrea, 'Mr. Clayton wants to see you.'

She was surprised. 'Right now?'

'He said as soon as you came down.'

'But I'm on duty. This is the busy time,' she protested.

Edna said, 'I imagine he knows that but maybe what he has to speak to you about is important. I can only tell you what he told me.'

Andrea still hesitated. 'It doesn't seem fair to you to have all the work. Surely he can wait.'

Edna looked concerned. 'He asked me to send you to his office at once.'

'Then I suppose I'd better go.'

'I would,' Edna agreed. 'Don't worry about in here. I've often handled it alone before. I don't say it's easy but I can do it.'

'Thanks,' she said absently, already wondering what the manager so urgently wished to see her about.

She left the dining room and went back to the lobby and down the short corridor to Ernest Clayton's office. The door was open but the office seemed empty. She knocked on the open door and waited.

A few seconds later he came down the corridor and joined her. 'Sorry,' he said apologetically. 'I was called to the front desk for a few minutes.'

'Edna said you wished to see me,' she said.

'Yes,' he agreed. 'Come on in.'

She went into the office with him and they sat. She told him, 'I was worried about leaving Edna alone to handle the dining room at this rush hour.'

The stout man eyed her solemnly. 'I appreciate that,' he said. 'But this is serious.'

'Oh?'

He ran a hand over his bald head and then opened a drawer of his desk and brought out a small, black object about one inch in diameter in every way. Handing her over the square, black object, he said, 'Have you ever seen this before?'

She took it and stared at it with puzzled eyes. It was of black plastic, very light, and had what seemed like the screened circular opening of a speaker on one side of it. There was also a tiny switch beside the speaker.

She shook her head. 'I've never set eyes on it before. What is it?'

Ernest Clayton was watching her closely. 'One of the maids came upon it by accident in your room. She had decided to move a bed aside to get at the carpet under it better. When she did she found this under the bed.'

She gave him a concerned look. 'You haven't told me what it is?'

'It's part of a two-way communication system,' he told her. 'The wireless type that need no wired connections. I've only seen a few of them. It appears that for some reason somebody has bugged your room.'

'Bugged my room?'

'Set up a listening post in it,' the manager told her. 'I have no idea where in the building the matched other half of this outfit might be. But it would appear that someone has been interested enough in any conversations taking place in your room to want to listen in on them.'

She was shocked. 'I can't imagine why!'

'Nor can I,' Ernest Clayton said with surprising sharpness. 'You're not in any trouble with the law are you, Miss Gibbs?'

'No!' she protested. 'What makes you think that?'

'I've known the police to use these things.'

'I've no police record of any kind,' she protested.

He looked somewhat relieved. 'I'm glad to hear that. But this still has to be explained. Can't you think why it should be in your room?'

'No,' she said. 'Not unless it has something to do with the silk-stocking murderer.'

The manager nodded. 'That occurred to me, also. If it should be some mad man there's no reason why he shouldn't use a knowledge of electronics to keep a close tab on you.'

'That's a frightening thought,' she said. 'And if it should be the answer it would eliminate any of the older suspects like Grant.' She could have added it also eliminated him from her suspicions.

'I wouldn't say that,' Ernest Clayton said grimly. 'Grant might get a listening set like this from somebody. I'm going to see that his room is checked for any such equipment—without his knowing it, of course.'

'Perhaps this may help to find the guilty person,' she said, handing the device back to him.

'A lot of the gamblers and bookies use such equipment,' the manager pointed out. He gave her another piercing look. 'You aren't in with any of those people, are you?'

Her cheeks burned. 'I'm not part of any crooked operation, Mr. Clayton.'

The stout man looked apologetic. 'Sorry,' he said. 'I'm just thinking of the hotel. I have to try and avoid any possible scandal.'

'I understand.'

'Nothing personal.'

'Of course not,' she said.

He held the speaker in his hand a moment and then put it back in his desk drawer and carefully locked the drawer. He told her, 'I'll talk to my friend on the police about this when I'm discussing that other business.'

She raised her eyebrows. 'You haven't seen him yet?'

The manager seemed uneasy. 'No. He has been busy and so have I.'

'I shouldn't think you'd lose any time.'

'I'll see that it's done,' he promised.

'So many things could happen in the interim,' she pointed out.

His face became stern. 'I must handle this in my own fashion. I am the one with the ultimate responsibility here.'

'Of course.'

'At least that thing is out of your room,' he said. 'So you can speak freely without being worried about being overheard.'

'I didn't worry before,' she said bitterly. 'I didn't know about it.'

'But it was there all the time.'

'So you say.'

252

'Any interesting conversations or phone calls you can think of?' he asked.

She knew there had been the call from David Barry, or at least whoever phoned in that muffled voice and claimed to be Barry. But she didn't want to tell him about it until after her meeting with the young newspaperman.

So she said, 'No. Everything was very routine.'

'I find this mysterious,' he said.

'I know. Is there anything else?'

'Not at the moment. You can return to your work.'

'Thank you,' she said, rising.

He gave her a look of curiosity. 'I hope this hasn't upset you too much.'

'No,' she said. 'It hasn't. Possibly because I've experienced so many upsetting things here already.'

Ernest Clayton's florid face shadowed. 'Yes. We have given you a rather bad time. Sorry.'

She left his office and returned to the dining room. Most of the patrons were already seated so she had it easy. Monty was seated at the piano and he gave her an interested look when she appeared. She was sure he'd be full of questions as to why she'd been called away. It was awkward. She wasn't sure she should tell him. What was his part in all this? He well might have put the listening object in her room.

When Monty finished at the piano he came out by her. He paused to ask, 'What's going on?'

She parried with, 'Clayton is worried about the reputation of the hotel again. He was asking me a lot more questions.'

'Has he talked with the police yet?'

'I don't think so.'

Monty was annoyed. 'I should think he'd do that rather than bother you with a lot more questions.'

'I agree.'

'Something odd about that Clayton.'

She smiled ruefully. 'He has stayed with the Ansonia too long. I notice even the guests who've been here for years tend to become a little odd.'

'No doubt about it,' the pianist said, surveying the dining room grimly. 'By the way I don't see Cal Wayne here tonight.'

'He doesn't always come in.'

'I'd expect him around on a day like this,' Monty said. 'He'll likely turn up in the lounge later. Are you coming in?'

'For a while,' she said. 'I'll have to leave around ten.'

'Oh?'

She quickly said, 'It's nothing important. I want to get to bed early.'

Monty relaxed. 'Then you'll be in for a while?'

'Likely,' she said.

He went back to playing the piano. And she noticed that Al Moroni and his henchman and girlfriend were at their table. They seldom missed a meal at the hotel. Seeing them made her wonder what game they might be playing in this city of riddles. It also struck her that Moroni would be the type to use sophisticated items like a wireless set for bugging rooms. And he'd seemed very pleased with himself the past few days. But why would he want to listen in on what she had to say?

She recalled that he'd let her know he considered her a friend of Cal Wayne's, having seen them together. Perhaps that could be the explanation. Moroni might have figured she was an accomplice of Cal Wayne's in some gambling game that was going on, and had bugged her room to find out about it. She should mention this to the manager and have him check Moroni's room and those of the other two with him. But she felt she should postpone doing this until she had a chat with Cal Wayne or kept her appointment with David Barry.

When she finished in the dining room she went into the lounge. There was an empty table for two near the bar and she took it. She'd barely been served a drink when Cal Wayne and Slim Gordon entered the lounge together. As soon as they saw her the two looked upset. The jockey murmured something to Cal and went on to take a stool at the bar while the young man with the dark glasses came straight to her table and sat down across from her.

'Good evening,' he said, mockingly.

'Good evening.'

'I understand you were very busy this afternoon.'

'I was.'

'Slim says you were out to the track to see him.'

She nodded. 'Yes. It was a waste of time.'

The man with the dark glasses smiled sourly. 'Didn't you know it would be?'

'I'd hoped he would talk to me.'

'About your David Barry?'

'Yes.'

'According to Slim you've already arranged to meet Barry. Why bother anyone else about him?'

'I feel there are things I'd like to know concerning him. Things he might not care to tell me himself.'

'Don't you trust Barry?'

'I think so.'

'Then why ask others for information he can best give you? Or are you bluffing about really having a meeting with him?'

She said, 'I'm going to see him.'

Cal Wayne said, 'How about taking me along?'

'I have to see him alone.'

'He wouldn't mind me,' Cal Wayne said

mockingly. 'And I'm anxious to have a chat with him.'

'What about?'

'A few items of interest.'

'I'll tell him,' she said.

'Do that,' Cal Wayne said. 'And in the meantime don't bother Slim or me with a lot of questions. I think you should find out about Barry directly from meeting him. Understand?'

'No.'

'You will,' he said, rising. 'I'd stay longer but I have a few things to attend to.' And with a humorless smile he went on to the bar and took the stool next to the jockey.

Monty was still presiding at the piano. The dimly lighted lounge was already well-filled. Then she saw Al Moroni and Rose come in. As they passed her Moroni noticed her and gave her an amused nod. Once again she had a feeling it was he who had placed the microphone in her room.

She watched as he and the dark girl sat together at a table only a short distance from her. There was no question that even though she dressed tastelessly Rose was beautiful. Andrea thought it sad that the girl wasn't making better use of the loveliness nature had bestowed on her.

She wondered where the third member of the trio, the battered Jake Gotell was? It was rare that Moroni appeared without him. She glanced at the bar and saw that Cal Wayne and his jockey friend were still there. She debated what the connection might be between them and the mysterious David Barry.

It had seemed wiser not to confide in Monty until after she met David Barry. She knew the pianist would be bound to raise a fuss about her going out alone to keep the rendezvous and then she still wasn't certain about him. Despite the fact that she liked him he had carefully kept himself a stranger to her. He'd not yet given her any real facts about his past.

She was thinking of all these things when Monty came back from his session at the piano. He smiled as he sat with her. He said, 'I see the entire cast of characters is here tonight. Moroni, the girl, Cal Wayne and Slim. What did Cal have to say to you?'

She grimaced. 'The usual nothing.'

'He lost no time in coming to this table,' Monty said.

'I know. I expected he'd have something important to tell me but he didn't.'

Monty glanced toward the bar. 'He's an oddball.'

'I agree.'

'And that jockey friend of his is no better.'

'They seem to suit each other,' she said. And then she frowned slightly. 'Do you smell anything funny?' she asked him.

'I don't think so.'

'I do,' she said. 'Smoke!'

'The place is full of cigarette smoke,' he told her glancing around at the crowded lounge.

'This is a different kind of smoke!' she insisted.

But before she could say anything more there was a loud scream of, 'Fire!' from the area of the lobby. At once the whole place was in a furor. The patrons jumped up and began milling about. Now there was no doubt that smoke was drifting in from the lobby. People began to cough and some were yelling.

Monty took up a stand by the emergency side exit and shouted for the patrons of the lounge to use that door to escape since it was impossible to go out through the lobby. Choking and stumbling, Andrea groped along with the others as they made their way out the single emergency exit. It seemed to take an endless time and the coughing and panic-stricken cries increased.

At last she staggered out into the alley which was now filled with people. She could hear the sound of fire engines drawing up in front of the hotel and a brief glance at the street gave her a glimpse of the revolving lights on the huge red trucks. The lights and clamor of the arriving fire department equipment increased the pandemonium.

She pushed her way through the milling crowd and tried to locate Monty. She didn't find him for several minutes and when she did he was kneeling by a woman who had

259

collapsed. He motioned Andrea over to him.

'What is it?' she asked kneeling beside him and taking a quick look at the pale, drawn face of the middle-aged woman stretched out on the asphalt.

'She has a bad heart,' Monty shouted in her ear, to be heard above the clamor. 'She took a nitro tablet but then she passed out. You watch her while I go for an ambulance.'

'All right,' she agreed breathlessly and took up a vigil by the stricken woman.

Monty vanished in the crowd. The shouts and general panic seemed to be continuing. After a moment a stout, middle-aged man came to join her. He knelt with her.

'I'm a doctor,' he said. 'They sent me here to see if there is anything to be done.'

'She seems to be breathing fairly regularly,' Andrea told him. 'And her heart beat isn't too bad.'

'You a nurse?' the doctor asked as he began to make an examination of the woman for his own information.

'No. But I've had first-aid training.'

He busied himself with tests for a minute. Then he told her, 'You'd gotten it all pretty straight. She seems to have survived the attack. But she should be sent to a hospital as soon as an ambulance arrives.'

'My friend has gone to get one,' she said.

The crowd in the alley thinned. Firemen rushed back and forth. And she learned from what she was able to hear that the fire had started in the kitchen and was now under control.

She was relieved to see Monty hurrying back. He told her, 'An ambulance is on the way.'

Andrea said, 'The doctor was here. He says she'll be all right.'

'I hope so,' the pianist said, kneeling alongside her. 'Thanks for taking over.'

'What about the fire?'

'It's out,' he said. 'Fat caught in the kitchen. They got it out without it spreading too far. The Ansonia survives to totter on in old age. Edna is out conferring with Ernest Clayton about how to keep the dining room service at normal.'

She shook her head. 'For a while I thought the hotel was doomed.'

'So did everyone.'

'You were wonderful getting people out,' she told him.

He smiled. 'I didn't think too much about it. It was the thing to do.'

The stretcher bearers and an intern arrived to take the woman. She and Monty drifted to the front of the hotel where the fire engines were still stationed. She saw with some amazement that the lobby had almost emptied of the thick smoke.

She said, 'The lobby looks a lot better.'

'No one will have to leave the hotel,' Monty

said. 'It will smell of smoke for a while but no serious harm seems to have been done.'

'Surely the lounge will close for the night,' she said.

He laughed. 'The way it emptied out I'd say the hotel lost a pot of money. It will take until the morning to get it cleaned up and straightened out.'

Edna separated from a group on the verandah and came down to join her. She said, 'I've talked with the cook and Ernest Clayton. There's enough equipment undamaged in the kitchen to keep the dining room going. But it will be an all-night job for the kitchen staff to get the place in shape.'

'I'm surprised the damage wasn't worse,' Andrea said.

'I know,' Edna agreed with a chuckle. 'I guess the Ansonia just won't be destroyed. You can imagine the time the manager is having trying to placate all those old ladies who were in their rooms. Most of them had to be helped out to the lawn in their nightgowns.'

Andrea said, 'I see they've gone back in now.'

Edna laughed. 'They'd rather suffer from the smoke than stand out here dressed as they were. We'll have checkouts in the morning. Most of them were scared stiff.'

She turned to say something to Monty and realized he had gone off somewhere. And it was only then that she looked at her watch and

262

saw that it was ten-thirty. She gave a gasp of dismay.

'I forgot all about the time!'

Edna stared at her. 'What does that mean?'

She gave the older woman a frantic look. 'I was supposed to meet someone at ten o'clock. It was important. And in the excitement I forgot it completely.'

'Well, no one would blame you for that!'

Andrea shook her head unhappily. 'This was a special kind of meeting. A secret meeting with someone I've been wanting to see. I was to be out by the stables at ten sharp.'

Edna looked surprised. 'By the stables?'

'Yes.'

'Whoever was to meet you probably came here to watch the fire,' she suggested.

'I don't think so,' she said unhappily. 'I'd better go now and see if he's still there.'

Edna stared at her. 'You're thinking of going out back there alone?'

'I must!' she said, turning to start on her way.

'Wait,' the older woman called after her. 'I can't let you do that. It would be foolhardy of you!'

She turned to her in desperation. 'But I promised.'

'Then it was a silly promise,' Edna told her. 'You know the things that have happened here!'

'I must go and find out if he's still there!'

she insisted.

'Then I'll go with you,' the white-haired woman said firmly.

'No,' she said. 'If he sees you he won't show himself.'

'I don't see why I should scare anyone,' Edna said. 'I'll keep a little distance behind you. But I won't let you go out there by yourself.'

Andrea realized that she was in a difficult position. She would have preferred to hurry out back to the stables area on her own and see if she'd missed David Barry. But now it was plain that Edna wouldn't let her do this. So the only alternative was to let the older woman accompany her.

With a sigh, she said, 'All right. He likely isn't there any longer. Keep a good distance behind me, please.'

'I don't want to interfere,' Edna said. 'I'll just keep you in sight, that's all. And if I see you are safe with someone I'll walk back to the hotel on my own. But I won't let you start out there by yourself.'

'You're too good,' she told her friend.

They started out to the back, circling the hotel and taking a path that led to the shuffleboard area and the several outbuildings beyond. The stables were the largest of the buildings and the most remote from the hotel. In the background the noise and excitement of the aftermath of the fire could still be heard.

But once they had gone as far as the shuffleboard part of the rear lawn it was pitch dark and very quiet. Andrea felt her nerves tense and she was suddenly glad to know that Edna was following behind her within calling distance. It was eerie out there by the deserted buildings.

Moving slowly so as not to stumble she reached the stables and stood waiting. For a moment she thought she heard a rustling sound to the left of her as if someone had moved and stepped on dry leaves but then there was only silence. She decided that it had been her imagination.

Edna was not in sight but she knew that the older woman could not be far away. And she did not feel that her presence would scare off the man she was supposed to meet there. He'd not know the white-haired woman was waiting a little distance back in the darkness.

She finally said aloud, 'David? David Barry? I'm waiting!'

There was no reply. She waited for perhaps three or four minutes before giving up. She knew that she should have been there on time if she'd expected to meet him. He wasn't likely to wait for her. He wouldn't want to take a chance of being discovered and so the fire would have chased him away. She had failed in meeting him for a second time.

Turning she walked back to the shuffleboard where she figured Edna stood waiting. 'No one there,' she said.

'I doubted if there would be considering the fire,' Edna said.

'We'd best go back to the hotel,' she told the older woman in a disappointed voice.

'I'm sorry,' Edna said.

'It's not your fault,' she replied as they started walking back in the darkness. 'I doubt if he would have been there even if I'd arrived at ten sharp.'

'Not likely. The fire broke out before then.'

Andrea said, 'I was glad to have you along. I can promise you that.'

'Never go out there alone after dark,' Edna warned her.

'I won't,' she said.

She was grateful that her friend made no inquiries about whom she had been going to meet or any of the details concerning the rendezvous. Together they entered the hotel where a harassed-looking Ernest Clayton was directing members of the staff in a cleaning-up operation. He kept shouting out his instructions and merely nodded to them as they passed.

Edna said, 'We'd better make up our minds to walk upstairs. There'll be no one operating the elevator tonight.'

'I know,' she agreed. And they began climbing the stairs. She said, 'I didn't see Olaf in the lobby.'

'You can bet he's in the kitchen where most

266

of the heavy work is to be done,' Edna commented. 'I guess we can do without a night watchman tonight. With all the activity going on downstairs we're not apt to get any intruders.'

She smiled. 'I wouldn't think so.'

They reached the fourth floor and said goodnight. Then Andrea started to unlock her door only to find that it was already unlocked. With an expression of surprise on her pretty face she opened the door to discover that the light was on in her room. And standing in the middle of the room under the dull glow of the single hanging bulb was a haggard-looking Grant!

CHAPTER TWELVE

Andrea stood there stunned as she stared at the elderly night clerk. All the suspicions she'd had of his being the silk-stocking murderer rushed into her mind. She was ready to hastily back out the door and scream for help in the hall. Edna could not yet have more than entered her room and so would be sure to hear her.

But before she could make a decision as to what to do the haggard Grant raised a hand in supplication. 'Please don't be frightened, Miss Gibbs,' he said in a weary voice. 'I'm here because I had to find a way to talk to you in private.'

Some of her fear drained away. She still hesitated in the doorway. She said, 'I'm surprised that you're not downstairs helping Mr. Clayton clean up after the fire.'

Grant's sallow face showed pain. 'I'm no longer with the hotel. After more than thirty-five years of service I've been dismissed. Clayton let me go earlier this evening before the fire.'

'Oh?'

Grant took a step toward her. 'I'm going to place my case before the owners and try and get my job back. It isn't worth much but it's all I can do. And you can help me.'

268

'I can?'

'Yes. The trouble began when Clayton had a police inspector come to my room here and question me. I knew what he was thinking right away. He was hinting that I was the original silk-stocking murderer and that I had killed that girl two years ago and the one last year. He even suggested that I had made attacks on you and you had identified me.'

She shook her head. 'That isn't true. Someone attacked me but I couldn't tell who it was.'

Grant's sunken face took on an eager look. 'If you stick by that story Miss Gibbs they'll have to give me back my job. They can't prove a thing against me.'

She stared at him wondering whether he were innocent or guilty. Certainly he wanted to be cleared in the matter. She said, 'I can't understand Mr. Clayton dismissing you so quickly.'

The old man looked embarrassed. 'It came about because I went down and accused him of trying to frame me. I told him he was no friend! That we'd worked together for the best part of a half-century and he'd tried to harm me!'

'I see.'

'I lost my temper and he lost his,' Grant went on. 'So that's how things stand now. I ask only that you tell the truth when you're questioned. I need to get my job back.'

'This is a bad night to discuss such things,' she said. 'Everything is in chaos because of the fire.'

Grant looked grim. 'Clayton deserved to have something like this happen. He's been getting by too easily. I could tell plenty of stories about him. Ask him about that Mrs. Flanders!'

She said, 'I don't think wild accusations are going to help any. If I were you I'd wait until all the fuss about the fire is settled and then apologize to Mr. Clayton. I feel sure he'll accept your apology and take you back. I'll speak to him on your behalf in the meantime.'

Grant said, 'Will you?'

'Yes. Since there seems to have been some misunderstanding about what I said to him about the attack on me, I want to clear that up.'

The former night clerk looked grateful. 'Thank you, Miss.'

'The best thing you can do for now is go to your room and get a good rest,' she suggested. 'I'm sure it will all work out in the morning.'

The haggard Grant moved to the door and out into the hallway. 'I hope so, Miss,' he said. 'I know nothing about those murders! None of them!'

She nodded and went inside and closed and locked the door. She left the key in the lock as an extra precaution. The hotel manager had said the locks were all old fashioned and so gave the hotel's patrons little security. No doubt Grant had had a master key, but whoever had hidden that microphone in her room must have also had a means of getting in. She doubted that it would be difficult for anyone who was determined to pick the lock.

Her room, like the rest of the hotel, smelled of smoke. She went to the window and opened it and decided to leave it open for the balance of the night. It had been a night of pandemonium and all her hopes of at last meeting the elusive David Barry had been dashed. Wearily she prepared for bed, her mind in a state of confusion. She turned out the lights and waited for sleep to come. It came after a long while.

But it was a restless sleep filled with troublesome dreams. She imagined herself being attacked in the darkness of the landing once again. She felt the rope looped around her neck and heard the heavy breathing of her killer!

The heavy breathing! She woke up full of fear and stared into the darkness. She was certain that she'd been awakened by that same sort of labored breathing!

Raising up on an elbow she peered into the shadows of her tiny bedroom and she was certain that she heard the door leading from the hallway creak closed. The sinister, scraping sound filled her with terror. She waited, frozen with fear, but nothing happened. At last she

271

lay back on her pillow and fell asleep again.

But in the morning she remembered those moments of horror. She carefully examined the door and found the key still in the lock. Yet she was sure she had heard the door open and close. It was a dull, cloudy morning with the promise of rain again and she wondered if the big raceway would have to cancel its racing schedule for the day.

She went downstairs to have breakfast at the staff table and noticed that the smell of smoke still clung to the old building. It was a miracle it had not gone up in flames. And she imagined everyone would be somewhat tense after the frightening experience.

Edna was busy showing someone to a table when Andrea entered the dining room. She went directly to the staff table and sat down. She'd only been there a few seconds when Edna came hurrying over to her. At once she noticed the white-haired woman was in a highly upset state and put it down to the fire of the previous night.

But as soon as Edna sat by her she heard the truth. The older woman said solemnly, 'I don't suppose you've heard what happened last night.'

She said, 'No. Unless you mean the fire.'

'Not the fire,' Edna said. 'There was another silk-stocking murder. That girl, Rose.'

The news stunned Andrea. 'Rose, murdered?'

'Yes,' Edna said soberly. 'The police have been here since the body was found around seven. They're with Ernest Clayton now.'

'I don't know what to say,' she managed.

'You'll be even more shocked when you hear where it happened,' Edna told her.

'Where?'

'By the stables. At almost the exact spot where you went to meet that man last night.'

Andrea couldn't speak for a moment. What she had heard was a confirmation of her worst fears. It seemed to surely mean that David Barry was the guilty party.

She gave Edna a frightened glance. 'You think?'

'I think the man you were planning to meet may have been her murderer,' Edna said. 'I'm glad I went out there with you. I may have saved you.'

'Yes,' she said in a whisper.

'That Rose must have gone out there while the hotel was on fire,' Edna continued. 'The police say she'd been dead for hours before she was found. And there was a blue silk stocking knotted around her throat!'

'How awful!'

'It can be a lesson to all of us. We've been getting too careless. And that killer, whoever he is, is still at large.'

'That's the dreadful part,' she said. 'What about Moroni and that other man who were always with Rose?'

273

'They've vanished The police are looking for them.'

'They don't suspect them of having anything to do with her death?'

'No. They think they're mixed up in some crooked dealings and don't want to be questioned. But the murder was in the same pattern of the other three. And the police think it was probably done by the same person.'

'It has to be a madman,' she said.

'Or the phantom,' Edna said dryly. 'And I don't think any ghost did it.'

'I'm afraid Mr. Clayton is going to have some bad publicity after all,' she said.

'No doubt about that. It may finish the hotel, between the fire and the scandal no one will want to stay here. I understand a half-dozen or more of the elderly women guests are already leaving this morning.'

'You can't blame them.'

Edna gave her a knowing look. 'I didn't say anything about our excursion to the stables last night when the police questioned me. I thought you might not want me to.'

'That was considerate of you.'

'You know the man you were to meet and he may be quite innocent of what happened. But if they knew he'd planned to be there they might suspect him.'

'True,' she agreed.

'You don't have to tell me who it was,' the

274

older woman said. 'But I would be careful in my future dealings with him if I were you.'

'You can depend on that.'

Edna got up. 'I won't take any more of your time. I know you haven't had breakfast.'

Andrea looked at her bleakly. 'I'm not certain I can manage any now.'

But she did remain at the table and have toast and then several cups of coffee. She sipped the hot liquid and sat there for a long while in a daze not knowing what she should do. It was while she was in this mood that the stout Ernest Clayton came into the dining room with his usually florid face pale and strained.

He came down to the staff table and said, 'I need some coffee.'

'Of course,' she said. And she poured him a cup of steaming black coffee from the percolator on the table.

The manager sat down and took a gulp of the hot drink without sugar or cream. Then he sat back and sighed. He glanced at her.

'You've heard?'

'Yes. I'm stunned.'

'Everyone is,' the manager agreed. 'I've just managed to get rid of the police for a little. They've gone back out again to look for more clues.'

She said, 'Will they want to question me? After all I was attacked several times. That was a warning for what happened last night.

It's just an accident the victim was Rose rather than me.'

The stout man ran a hand over his bald head in a nervous gesture. 'Because I didn't report those attacks at the time I didn't say anything at all to the police about them now. If I had they would have blamed me for not calling them in.'

She gave him a shocked look. 'Isn't that concealing vital information?'

'I don't know. I only know I can't mention any of it.'

'But you told your inspector friend. He questioned Grant.'

The manager looked surprised. 'You know that?'

'Grant told me. He came to my room last night and asked me to help him get his job back.'

Ernest Clayton looked angry. 'The nerve of him!'

'He meant no harm.'

'That's what you think,' the manager raged. 'I wish I could be as sure.'

She said, 'So at least one member of the police knows about the attacks.'

'I called him in as a private investigator,' the manager said. 'I bound him to secrecy. He won't reveal any of that to the police department.'

Andrea said, 'In that case you'd better be quick to make your peace with Grant or he'll give the whole show away. He's going to appeal to the owners of the hotel and the police on the grounds that you have no evidence against him. He wants his job back and I'd say you should give it to him.'

'He insulted me or I wouldn't have fired him!'

'Better forget that. I told him I'd speak on his behalf and if he apologized you'd likely take him back.'

The manager stared at her. 'You know what you're saying? And you also know that he may have done all the murders, the one thirty-five years ago and these other three?'

'You have no proof.'

'It may turn up.'

'Time to dismiss him then,' she said.

The manager drank some more of the coffee and she saw that his hand was trembling. He said, 'I'll have to take him back. He's in a position to blackmail me.'

'That's largely your own fault.'

The stout man looked miserable. 'The fire wasn't calamity enough! Now to have something like this happen!'

'You should have called the police in earlier,' she said. 'I'm sorry but that's what I honestly think.'

He looked at her nervously. 'Can I count on you to keep quiet about the attacks on you? Otherwise I'll definitely be in bad trouble.'

'I'll say nothing for the moment,' she said.

'But I won't promise not to talk if there is any more violence.'

'Surely they'll find the murderer this time!'

'You really think so?'

He sighed dejectedly. 'I don't know. Rose was an underworld character. It's hard to know what enemies she had. If only she hadn't been throttled silk-stocking style it would probably have been put down as an underworld killing. Especially since Moroni and that Jake Gotell have vanished.'

'The murderer seems to enjoy leaving his trademark.'

'Yes.'

She said, 'Perhaps it is a ghost after all. Why would any real criminal deliberately leave something to associate him with all the other crimes?'

'He has to be mad,' the manager said. 'And after last night I think Grant is not completely sane.'

She warned him. 'He's not too sold on you either. And he seems to know a few scandalous things about you to back up his opinion. I'd say you can't afford a quarrel with him.'

The manager downed the rest of his coffee at a gulp. He gave her an annoyed look. 'Thanks,' he said. And he got up and strode out of the dining room.

She remained at the table only a few minutes after he left. Then she went out into the lobby. The elderly woman desk clerk was having a difficult time trying to settle the checks of three of the ancient women guests who were leaving. They were all talking loudly and seemed to want to have the various bills looked after at one and the same time. The elderly woman clerk was screaming back at them. It was a scene delicately balanced between comedy and tragedy.

Andrea moved on across the lobby and came upon Olaf laboriously mopping up the floor. He paused in his work to give her a doleful glance from behind his thick glasses.

'I was not on guard last night,' he said in his sing-song tone. 'But I will be with you tonight. You do not need to be afraid.'

'I'm glad to hear that after what happened out by the stables last night,' she said.

The big man nodded solemnly. 'Another murder.'

'Isn't it terrible!' she lamented. 'That poor girl!'

The big man shrugged. 'I did not know her. But I guard the hotel well every night. Last night it was the fire made me stay in the kitchen.'

'I know,' she said. 'You mustn't feel badly about it. She went out there alone in the dark and you can hardly be held responsible for that.'

She moved on to let him continue his work. To get away from the smell of smoke she went out to the rear verandah which was deserted due to the cloudy weather and the general panic in the old hotel.

And she now began to wonder how Rose had happened to go out by the stables. She had not told anyone of her rendezvous with David Barry out there except Edna. So Rose must have ventured out to the deserted buildings in the dark for some reason of her own. Perhaps she'd been caught and killed somewhere else and her body merely left there.

She heard someone come up behind her and turned with a start. Then she relaxed. It was Monty. She said, 'I wondered where you were.'

Monty was dressed in a white turtleneck and dark blue slacks. He gave her an angry look. 'Where did you vanish to last night?'

'What do you mean?'

'I left you for a moment and when I came back you had gone. And I wasn't able to find you again.'

She had to lie to him about going out to the stables. She said, 'I went into the hotel and upstairs to bed.'

Monty eyed her reproachfully. 'You might have at least let me know.'

'I intended to but you were so long getting back.'

'You just imagined that.'

Monty said, 'You know Rose was

murdered?'

'Yes. How awful!'

'Considering the attacks made on you I wasn't too surprised,' he said.

'Clayton withheld that information from the police. Now he's in a panic.'

'He has a right to be,' Monty said with a scowl. 'He's partly responsible for last night's murder.'

She was impressed by his show of indignation. And she recalled that once she had been sure that he was the mad killer. But unless he was a superb actor she was certain that she must have been badly wrong.

She said, 'Have you seen Cal Wayne this morning?'

'No. I wonder about him.'

'So do I.'

'He and Moroni were apparently enemies. It could be that he knows more about Rose's murder than the rest of us.'

She gave the young pianist a troubled look. 'You honestly think that?'

'Wayne is a strange character.'

'I agree. I don't understand him. But I think I know people in a general way. I can't picture him as a murderer.'

'Doesn't mean a thing,' Monty said. 'I'm sure there were people who offered character references for Bluebeard. Murderers are the most deceptive of all criminals.'

'And everyone has a theory as to who the

silk-stocking killer must be, ranging from Grant to the ghost of James Dennis.'

'It's likely the madman who did it will get away with it again,' Monty said. 'This should be your cue to leave.'

'I can't.'

'Because you haven't found David Barry?'

'Yes.'

'Forget it,' the young man said scornfully. 'I doubt if he'll ever turn up. And remaining here could cost you your life.'

'Then I'll have to risk it,' she said. 'Olaf will be on guard again beginning tonight. He's promised to keep a special watch on me.'

Monty looked gloomy. 'Olaf means well,' he said. 'But he is old and slow-witted. I don't consider him a proper person to be on guard here. He'd never be able to deal with the clever killer we're up against. Someone really wily!'

'He's dependable and very strong,' she said.

'What's the use,' the pianist said. 'You won't listen to reason! All right! Stay on here! See what happens to that tender neck of yours! You've had two escapes! The third time you'd better not count on being so lucky!' And he turned and headed back inside.

'Monty!' she called after him, but he didn't hear her or if he did, refused to pay any attention.

She remained on the verandah feeling miserable. She stared out across the lawn and beyond the shuffleboard area. She could see the police roaming about in the bushes by the stables in a search for clues. What a grisly business!

It began to rain around two o'clock. It was mostly showers and she heard that the racing had not been cancelled. She was not too busy at noon and she missed Moroni, his henchman and the beautiful Rose. It was hard to believe the pretty dark girl was stretched out on a slab in the Albany mortuary.

In the afternoon she slept. And she returned to the dining room at six in time for the dinner guests. There weren't many. A number of guests had checked out of the hotel and word of the murder and the fire kept away a majority of the transients who just dropped in for a meal. They were able to close the dining room early.

Edna had little to say. The lobby was almost deserted. Monty had merely nodded to her in the dining room and now he'd moved on to the lounge. Gloom hung over the old hotel like a grim shadow.

She debated whether to go up to her room or to go to the lounge. In the end she decided in favor of the lounge. It was possible that Cal Wayne might show up there and she badly wanted to see him. She was going to question him about David Barry again and hope for some direct answers.

When she got to the lounge she found

plenty of empty tables. The fire had taken its toll of the lounge business as well. She sat at a table near the lobby entrance and from there she could watch Monty. She was sure he saw her but he stubbornly avoided looking her way. It was a new attitude on his part.

She ordered a drink. And when time came for Monty to take his break she expected him to come and talk to her. Instead he vanished in some other area of the lounge. It was another rebuke which stung her. She remained at the table and he came back again to play another set of tunes. She occupied herself by playing a game of trying to catch his eye.

Absorbed in this she didn't notice that someone had come to stand beside her. And when she looked up she was shocked to find herself staring into the angry face of Al Moroni.

In a soft voice the gangster said, 'I don't want you to make a sound. I've got a gun pointed at you through my coat pocket. If you so much as move wrong I'll let you have it. Now, I want you to get up and leave here with me.'

She knew by the menace in his voice that he meant everything he said. She merely gave a frightened nod and rose from the table. They walked out into the lobby together. The waiter would not worry about her leaving without paying as he knew she was staff and would expect her back. At the moment she felt it was dubious if she'd ever be back alive.

The lobby was empty of people so there was no one to see her plight. They went out the front doors and down the steps to a car that was waiting. Moroni opened the door and nodded for her to get in. She did and he followed quickly. As he sat beside her and shut the car door she noticed that Jake Gotell was driving.

Moroni snapped at him, 'All right! Get going!'

Gotell said nothing but drove away from the hotel at a fast clip. Moroni had removed the gun from his pocket and now she saw its shining steel and ugly muzzle pointed at her.

'Why?' she asked frantically.

'To even things for Rose maybe,' Moroni said.

'I had nothing to do with that!' she protested.

Moroni smiled coldly as the car moved rapidly along one of the Saratoga streets. 'You planted that bit about meeting David Barry at ten by the stables. You knew we'd bugged your room and would hear it. You set Rose up for Barry to kill her!'

'No!' she cried. 'You're wrong!'

Moroni said, 'You can save your life if you tell us where Barry is hiding out now and what he did with the stuff.'

'I don't know what you're talking about!'

The swarthy man lifted his hand and

deliberately struck her across the face. It was a stunning blow and she fell back. She began to sob and felt the bitter taste of salt from a bleeding lip.

'Your memory improving any?' Moroni asked.

'I've never met David Barry,' she cried. 'I don't know what he looks like!'

'What now?' Jake Gotell asked from the front seat.

'We'll take her to the shack,' Moroni said. 'She needs time to work on her memory.'

'Okay,' the man at the wheel said as they sped on through the darkness of the side road they'd taken after leaving the city.

Moroni told her, 'You're making it tougher for yourself. We are going to get Barry and there's nothing you can do to stop us. He and Slim Gordon have the stuff and we aren't leaving Saratoga without it!'

Dazed and sobbing she huddled in a corner of the car's near dark rear seat. She had no idea how long they drove or where they were taking her. Suddenly the car came to a screeching halt on gravel.

Moroni took her roughly by the arm. 'Get out,' he said.

Gotell had opened the car door for them and they stumbled out into the cool blackness of the night. Moroni led her forward to what she made out as a tumbledown, unpainted barn. Gotell was ahead with a flashlight. He unlocked a plain door near the end of the barn and Moroni shoved her inside.

Moroni told her, 'The rats like this place so you'll have plenty of company. We'll be back in a couple of hours and maybe you'll feel more like talking by then!'

'Please!' she begged the two.

Their reply was coarse laughter. She had a brief look at the single big room without furniture or windows by the glow of the flashlight. Then the two went out and locked the door after them leaving her terrified in the darkness. Their mention of rats crossed her mind and she ran to the door and pounded on it, pleading for them to let her out. The next sound she heard was the car driving away!

Eyes wide with terror she stood with her back against the door facing the darkness of the room. The darkness and the menace! She knew she must somehow fight for courage to stand the ordeal ahead. There was no telling how long it might be before the two returned. They would stay away long enough for her nerves to crack. That would be their hope!

Long minutes passed and she remained almost motionless. Then she heard the first rustling sound not far from her. She tensed just as there was a tiny squeak and a scampering across the floor only a foot or so away from her. The rats!

'No!' she screamed and tried to control her sobbing.

She was still sobbing when she heard the sound of a car puffing up and decided the two had come back. Now she was too sick with terror to know what to say.

Then there was a pounding on the door and she heard a familiar voice cry out, 'Andrea! Are you in there?'

It was Monty! She turned and began pounding frantically on the door on her side, terrified that he might not hear her. 'Yes! Please help me! Get me out of here!'

'All right,' he called back. 'Give me a moment to get a stone big enough to break that door!'

Then there was silence and she heard the thin whimpering sounds and fresh scurrying as the rats in the dark room became bolder. She cried out Monty's name and begged him to hurry. It was only seconds later that he attacked the door and she felt it shudder and splinter a little.

'Stand away!' he warned her as he continued to assault the door with the rock or whatever he'd found. It took several minutes before it sagged away and he was able to force it open.

'How did you find me?' she moaned as she stumbled into his arms.

'I saw Moroni take you out. I left the piano right then and there,' he said, his arms around her. 'Then I followed their car in mine. I happened to be parked right near the door so I lost no time. But I had to keep a distance away so they wouldn't get wise I was after them. Next I lost them on a side road. But I finally wound up here and decided it looked like a probable spot to keep you a prisoner.'

She shook her head. 'In there! Rats!'

'I'm not surprised,' he said. 'Now let's get away from here before they return.'

Not until they were in Monty's car and well on the way back to Saratoga did she feel anything like herself. She said, 'They are after David Barry and that jockey. And they talked about "stuff." It must be some kind of dope racket!'

'No doubt,' Monty said at the wheel. 'It should cure you of David Barry.'

'I can't understand it. He was a respectable newspaperman,' she said. 'Rose went out to meet him and it seems he killed her.' She paused. 'I think Cal Wayne is really David Barry and our killer.'

'Wouldn't surprise me,' Monty said as they drove along Union Avenue.

'You'll lose your job leaving the lounge like that,' she said.

He gave her a grimly amused look. 'Is that important now?'

'I suppose not,' she said. 'Where are we going?'

'Back to the hotel. We'll have to risk it for tonight. And tomorrow you return to New York.'

'I guess I should,' she said. 'The police will have to know about Moroni.'

'I'll take care of that,' Monty promised her. 'Right now I want to escort you up to that hotel room of yours and see you safely locked in.'

And that was what he did. He left her to go tell his story to the police. It was agreed she'd see the police herself before she left for New York City in the morning. She was still in a shattered state and even the dingy old hotel seemed warm and inviting after what she'd been through.

Slowly she prepared for bed. She felt now that she'd very likely not ever have a face-to-face meeting with David Barry. She had even lost her desire to. It was almost certain he was a crook or an accomplice of crooks and even a killer. The computer dating prank had brought her to a sorry plight.

She was about to put out the light and get into bed when she heard slow footsteps outside in the corridor. Then there was a knock on the door.

'Yes?' she said in a frightened voice.

'It is only me, Olaf,' came the comforting reply. 'You are all right?'

'Yes. Thank you. Good to know you are on the job.'

'Yes, Miss,' Olaf said in his sing-song fashion. 'Mr. Clayton has asked me to look in every room to make sure no one has hidden in them. Would you let me in for a moment?'

'Of course,' she said, reaching for her robe. 'But I'm sure I'm quite alone.'

'Best to double check,' Olaf told her. 'After last night.'

'You're so right,' she said and opened the door for him.

The big man gave her a reassuring smile as he came in. He had a flashlight in his hand. 'I'll just look in the closet,' he said and moved toward it as she watched.

She thought how wrong Monty was about him. Olaf was slow but he was thorough. He'd even closed the door after him when he'd entered her room. Now he was taking his time searching in the closet. His back was still to her.

She smiled and said, 'No one there?'

'No one there,' he agreed and turned to her again. He had that pleasant smile on his battered face but the flashlight was no longer in his hand. Instead he was holding a silk stocking in both hands and still smiling as he was advancing slowly toward her.

She screamed as she realized she was cut off from escaping by the door. In the same instant he was on her, breathing heavily, and looping the silk stocking expertly around her neck. He laughed as he drew it tight. But he never did get it as tight as he wished for at that moment the door burst open and the room filled with police.

Olaf gave a wild cry and sprang away from them. A shot rang out as one of the police fired at him. But he'd already plunged out through the window! Andrea, on the floor and leaning against the bottom of her bed, took all this in rather stupidly. Then she fainted.

When she came to she was in a hospital room. A nurse was smiling down at her and she saw that it was morning. The nurse told her, 'As soon as the doctor sees you and says you're all right I have two interesting visitors for you.'

Propped up on pillows she received the visitors about a half hour later. One of them was Monty Freeman and the other was Cal Wayne, without his dark glasses for once.

Smiling, he told her, 'Let's get it over with. I'm David Barry.'

'I guessed that,' she said, staring at him. 'And you're not a crook or a killer?'

'I hope not,' the young man said.

'What about Olaf?' she asked.

Monty Freeman replied, 'Olaf is dead. He died from the fall. There's no doubt now that not only did he do the last three silk-stocking murders but the one thirty-five years ago as well. It seems he was working here part time when the first murder occurred. No one thought good-natured Olaf could have had anything to do with it. They didn't realize he was mad. And so my father went to prison for the crime.'

'Your father?' she gasped.

Monty nodded. 'Yes. I'm one of James Dennis's sons. I came back here because the killings had resumed and I hoped to prove my father's innocence. That's why I took the job at the hotel.'

'And you did prove his innocence,' she told Monty. 'We know now it wasn't his ghost who'd come back to do the murders *or* any new killer. But Olaf returned to the scene of his first crime and mad enough to continue killing.'

Monty sighed. 'I'm glad it's over.'

From the other side of the bed David Barry smiled and said, 'I haven't had a chance to tell my story yet.'

She gave him a wry look. 'I'd like to hear that. I'd like it very much. I'd especially like to know why you brought me on this mad chase here. Why did you disappear and wind up in Saratoga?'

'Not for the races, I promise you,' the handsome man said. 'When I first started writing to you I had every intention of getting in touch with you. Then just as we were to meet I stumbled on a big story. A man I knew who'd owned a racing stable and lost it phoned me in a bad state of fright. He confessed that he'd gotten mixed up in drug peddling and had a huge amount of the stuff in his apartment. He wanted to get out of the racket and asked my help as a go-between with the police. He felt as a newspaperman I could do this.'

She said, 'Did you go to his apartment?'

'Yes. But when I got there he had already been killed by one of his partners who made off with the parcel of drugs. I was in the apartment with the dead man when Al Moroni and his pal arrived. They got a look at me but I managed to get out of the apartment by a rear fire escape. From then on I was a hunted man. They figured that I'd killed the owner of the apartment and had taken the drugs.'

'So you decided to get out of town?' she said.

'The paper gave me leave. It's been a big story. I had an idea the man who'd done the murder and taken the drugs had come to Saratoga. I didn't know the town well but I had a jockey friend here, Slim Gordon. And he introduced me around as a small time gambler.'

'Then Moroni arrived still looking for you and the drugs?' Andrea said.

'Right. I tried to persuade you to leave Saratoga. I made those phone calls and I argued with you as Cal Wayne. But you wouldn't listen.'

She grimaced. 'I was too interested in David Barry. And what did that get me? Kidnapped by Moroni and locked in a barn full of rats!'

'I'm sorry,' David Barry said. 'If it's any comfort to you the police have Moroni and Gotell along with the man who did the murder in New York and took the drugs. They have the dope as well.'

'I'm thrilled,' she said with acid humor. 'And I find it interesting that you, who got me in all this trouble, are still in the best of physical shape, while I'm in a hospital bed.'

'Sorry,' David Barry said. 'Think of it this way. You helped in cracking a drug ring and a murder case and have seen all the criminals caught for their crimes.'

'That does help some,' she admitted. 'So we meet at last.'

David Barry smiled. 'But not for long. I have to rush back to New York to file my story in detail. But we will meet again. We have to.'

'No,' she said, raising a hand. 'Don't plan on it. Not even after all those romantic letters we exchanged.'

David Barry glanced across her bed to Monty and winked. Then he told her, 'About those letters. They were great. But I don't think we'd ever get along person to person. And I'm especially sure of it since I've seen you get along so well with a certain other person since you've been here.'

Andrea looked at Monty and blushed. 'For a time I thought you were a murderer,' she confessed.

The good-looking pianist said, 'And I thought you were terribly stupid. And we were both wrong. So let's begin again.'

'I think I'd like that,' she agreed with a

smile.

Monty, always the man of action, at once leaned forward and took her in his arms for a lasting kiss. When they finally parted she looked around, startled. 'What about David?'

Monty laughed. 'I'm afraid he's vanished again!'

She gazed around the empty hospital room. Then she turned to Monty once more. 'This time it doesn't matter,' she said. And he took her in his arms again.

We hope you have enjoyed this Large Print book. Other Chivers Press or Thorndike Press Large Print books are available at your library or directly from the publishers.

For more information about current and forthcoming titles, please call or write, without obligation, to:

Chivers Large Print
published by BBC Audiobooks Ltd
St James House, The Square
Lower Bristol Road
Bath BA2 3BH
UK
email: bbcaudiobooks@bbc.co.uk
www.bbcaudiobooks.co.uk

OR

Thorndike Press
295 Kennedy Memorial Drive
Waterville
Maine 04901
USA
www.gale.com/thorndike
www.gale.com/wheeler

All our Large Print titles are designed for easy reading, and all our books are made to last.